Night of Confusion

Down the "Slot"—that fabled channel between chains of islands in the Solomon group—steamed the task force of Admiral Gunichi Mikawa, Japanese Imperial Navy.

His target: the Allied cruiser group gathered off Savo Island, near Guadalcanal.

Three thousand Japanese guns were pointed at the destroyer **Blue**, on interception duty at the head of the Allied column. But no one aboard **Blue** noticed the enemy force churning past—so **Blue** roused no enemy fire.

Not so lucky were the cruisers **Quincy, Vincennes, Canberra** and **Astoria.** This exciting factual book details the incredible confusion and horror that made the Battle of Savo a low point in American naval history.

THE BATTLE OF SAVO

by
STAN SMITH

WILDSIDE PRESS

TO MY SON, JOHN

Acknowledgments

I am deeply indebted to Mr. Dean Allard, Naval Research Center; Lieutenant Commander Frederick H. Prehn, USN and Yeoman Second Class Anthony Metro, USN, Navy Magazine and Book Branch; and Miss Molly Thompson, Australian Consulate Library, for their kindness and unstinting assistance in the preparation of this book. My gratitude also to certain individuals for their recounting of incidents in the Battle of Savo, in which they took part.

New York   Stan Smith
April, 1962

CHAPTER 1

THE WEEK of August 8-15, 1942, moved in massive paradox for the American public. At Pearl Harbor Navy Yard, tall, white-haired Admiral Chester W. Nimitz, Commander in Chief of the Pacific Fleet, released on August 8 the news that United States Marines had landed in the remote Solomon Islands. There had been no good war news since the Battle of Midway two months earlier—only gloomy reports of U-boat sinkings and Russian reverses on the Black Sea.

"A concentration of the forces of the United States Pacific Fleet, with units at Pearl Harbor, and the Pacific Command, operating from Australia," announced Admiral Nimitz, "combined yesterday in an attack on Japanese positions in the Tulagi area of the Solomon Islands. Operations are proceeding favorably, despite opposition of enemy land-based aircraft and garrisons."

The press responded accordingly. Banner headlines blanketed the nation.

For America it was the first decent report since June 4, when United States Navy carriers had turned back the Japanese Navy—had, in fact, routed it decisively.

Few who read those initial reports from Pearl Harbor were alarmed by a simultaneous Tokyo Radio newscast, heard in London, reporting a uniquely different version of the same story:

"Imperial Japanese Headquarters announced today that our naval units have attacked the American Fleet which appeared near the Solomon Islands, inflicting heavy damages on enemy warships as well as transports. The attack is being continued. Enemy warships sunk: one battleship, size unascertained; two heavy cruisers of the *Astoria* type; more than three heavy cruisers, type unascertained, and more than ten transports."

If anything, the "absurdity" of these enemy claims tended only to make the newscasters downgrade the importance of the whole story. Nobody seemed worked up or curious; nobody

7

demanded an inquiry. A terse statement from stolid General Douglas MacArthur in Australia provided the necessary public reassurance:

"The air forces are attacking vigorously and are cooperating with the United Nations naval forces by making heavy raids on Japanese bases."

The Jap claims are "preposterous," the commentators said mightily in passing. The Jap must save face. "He's prone to exaggeration and distortion." Which he was, to a point, the commentators continued.

The New York *Times* of Sunday headlined the invasion story in an edition which also spoke of an Aleutians attack by the Navy, Ghandi's arrest, and the execution of six Nazi saboteurs. And since few readers knew the whereabouts of the Solomons, a distant Pacific chain, a map was reproduced beside the front-page story. For the first time Choiseul, Malaita, Santa Isabelle, Russells, Rendova, Savo, Tulagi and Guadalcanal appeared before the public.

Guadalcanal, in particular, would stick in the nation's eye like a sliver of green glass. Here would be the scene of a savage and unremitting struggle, and a place of disease and death. This lump of emerald hell was the grotesque prize for which six major naval engagements would be fought, in addition to the campaigns of the Marine Corps. Guadalcanal would continue to make news for more than a year, just as surely as the name Savo would be transmuted to Ironbottom Sound by the United States Navy.

Before the taxpayer allowed himself to think about validity of Japanese claims, however, he wanted to dream of winning for just a bit. Pearl Harbor still tingled in his ears. He wanted to stretch his imagination out to that Pacific area and conjure up a few well-meaning hallucinations—laughing natives sailing outrigger canoes before the gentle trades; copper-skinned sylphs with flowers in their hair. The lyric sensuality of the Solomon Islands captured his imagination as he pored over the first battle reports, and he cared not a whit for Japanese assertions.

That dynamo of the Mutual network, Gabriel Heater, cried: "Our boys are fighting! The Pacific Fleet is in business!"

It surely was, and the business was hotter than anyone suspected.

On Monday, August 10, the New York *Times* reported still another Tokyo Radio broadcast heard in London:

"The Imperial Japanese Navy has sunk a battleship, two

10,000-ton cruisers of the *Astoria* type, two Australian cruisers of the *Australia* type, three other cruisers, at least four destroyers, and more than ten transports."

The American public had already, during this war, arrived at the conclusion that it was not possible to have an invasion without some losses. The public didn't especially want to be told about these losses, but city editors did. And so the questions started. By Monday night there were additional Japanese claims, and newsmen disregarded protocol and asked the Navy Department pointed questions. Have we, they asked, suffered losses, and if so to what extent? Was it all true that a major night engagement had been fought? Where did the Nip come off saying he had kicked hell out of the United States Navy?

For a few hours these questions remained unanswered, the result of which was simply to whet the newsmen's curiosity and voraciousness (Admiral King's word). Then, much later that day, the Navy Department issued a statement:

"The offensive operation 'in force' of the United States naval and other units against the Japanese installations in the southwestern section of the Solomon Islands was reported as continuing. Considerable enemy resistance has been encountered, and it is still too early to announce results of our own or the enemy losses. . . ."

Admiral King, who personally thought precious little of newspapers except that "they have a way of cluttering up things," had told them approximately nothing. But the following morning, Tuesday, August 12, the New York *Times* remarked:

"Neither from the War or Navy Department was it possible to elicit a denial."

Australian Prime Minister John Curtain was interviewed on Wednesday. He had even less to say than King.

But on August 15, Curtain tersely avowed that "we are holding our own."

A news clampdown concerning events at Savo Sound off Guadalcanal was put into immediate effect, and the American public quietly resigned itself to *some* losses off the Solomons.

Two months later, on October 12, the Navy Department released Official Communique 147:

"Certain initial phases of the campaign not announced previously for military reasons can now be reported," it began.

It proceeded to give a clear, factual account, without excuses, of the sinking of the heavy cruisers *Astoria, Quincy,*

Vincennes and the Australian heavy cruiser *Canberra* in Savo Sound, by an enemy task force that first night when Marines were ashore in the Solomons. Three other ships had been damaged, and the death toll—not released until after the war—stood at 1,024.

So began a controversy which was to last for some sixteen years; cause unspeakable embarrassment at the Navy Department and the suicide of one of the officers involved; and be a hotly debated issue at open forum and in the press. There were *two* Pearl Harbors, decided a San Francisco newspaper, and the other was Savo.

"It was one of the worst defeats ever inflicted upon the United States Navy," wrote historian Samuel Eliot Morison.

Down from Bougainville for about 600 miles, the Solomons form a double strand of emerald islands which extend to San Cristobal in a southwesterly direction below the equator and approximately northwest of Australia. Between these strands runs a deep water channel called "The Slot," so named by American sailors who fought in the South Pacific.

Alvarado Medana, a cousin of the King of Spain, his sponsor, discovered the islands in 1567 and lived to regret it, although at first the discovery had elated him. Medana believed the islands were the site of Ophir, the Biblical land of gold; and, being a real estate developer of sorts, he planned to exploit the potential to its fullest by convincing the King that mining and colonization expeditions be sent out. The Spaniard named the first of the islands in this chain Santa Isabelle. He named one of the last Guadalcanar, and the original spelling persisted as late as the twentieth century. It was an immense island, jungle-fringed and volcanic, with a string of ominous mountains rising out of ridges in the background.

Guadalcanar, frequently discussed in Jack London's writings, was an island of dialects and passions—eighteen dialects and a universal passion for human heads. After planting the flag on every bit of sod he found, Medana returned to Spain. However, internal problems and small wars relegated the explorer and his discovery to obscurity. Nobody particularly cared about the Solomons for a while.

Twenty-seven years later, Medana again received his King's blessings. On his second trip the explorer took four ships, 400 prospectors, and a wife. But now he couldn't find the Solomon Islands. Actually he had come as far as the Santa

Cruz chain, somewhat short of the mark, but he searched around for two months without losing hope. One of the causes of great concern to Medana was a threatened mutiny. Another was the loss of one of his ships, the *Santa Isabella,* during a storm.

Heartbroken and baffled, Medana died at Santa Cruz, where the expedition had stopped to fill the casks. He was buried on the island.

There was no more talk of the Solomon Islands for two centuries. Then, in rapid succession, Bougainville and Shortland rediscovered them. It was about this time that the quaint customs of the Melanesian natives began to come to light. Head-hunting and cannibalism were the hallmark of the Solomons. In 1838 *Annales Maritime* mentioned shipwrecks and ransom, in an article concerning the type of hospitality one might expect:

> "A considerable number of shipwrecks are being held captive, in many islands, by the natives. Most of the prisoners are American or British. After being wrecked by furious tropical storms in these islands, they have lost every semblance of liberty and in many places have been subjected to the greatest of privation and the most savage treatment."

The Frenchman D'Utriville wrote in 1852:

> "Two canoes, containing about twelve men, had ventured fairly close, but without attempting to come alongside. It was noticed that two of the men in the canoe wore belts resembling those of officers' uniforms in Europe. They were making gestures like those of a man requesting a shave. Several of the natives had pieces of red and blue cloth attached to their garments, thus proving that they had been in touch with Europeans."

Warned by such stories, the rest of the world wanted little to do with the Solomon Islands.

"It is a place of death," Jack London wrote. United States Marines used more graphic language. It was a place of shoals and shipwrecks, and of hideous and pagan people. Only a few sailors continued to come to the Solomons, and the ones who escaped with their lives did their utmost to perpetuate the stories of native barbarism.

The Solomons lay abandoned by the world until about

the time of the John Rushworth Jellicoe tour after World
War 1. The famed British admiral, making an inspection tour
of the Pacific, saw the wide blue harbor of Tulagi and realized
the value of a Royal Navy station there. Soon after, the island
became a British protectorate. With this also came an adminis-
tration, a resident commissioner, an Anglican bishop, and the
first few whites, who were either prospectors or drunks.

Melanese character and customs underwent a remarkable
transformation now. These short, muscular black men who
had carved up strangers for centuries enlisted in the island con-
stabulary to enforce British laws.

The Thirties brought a few more whites to the Solomons
to staff a radio station, which was government controlled, and
a Royal Australian Air Force base. It was during this period
of expansion that large plantations, such as those of Lever
Brothers and Burns Philp, were established. These plantations
served as the principal trading posts. On Tulagi was a good
beach, a clubhouse for military personnel, and a Chinatown.

The town was a one-street, two-bar affair, with a number of
ramshackle corrugated iron houses, and two broken-down
hotels. One of the bars was called Sam Doo's—according to
the coastwatcher, Feldt, who lived in these islands for years.
Predominantly Chinese, with a smattering of whites and Mela-
nesians, the town offered a decadent hospitality to strangers
passing through. And almost everybody *passed* through. No
large group of people had come to settle the island since 1865,
when the cutter *St. Paul* piled up on the rocks off Savo and
400 Chinese, unquestionably the forebears of the 1942 resi-
dents, came ashore.

Across the water was Guadalcanal, a land of copra plantations and prospectors. The native population of this island was
several thousand, while at Malaita some 14,000 had been reg-
istered by an Australian census. But few could abide the damp
heat of malaria-infested Guadalcanal and its plains of six-foot-
tall kunai that stretched out for miles. Few tried.

It was a big island, almost 90 miles long by 25 wide. In the
background, rising 6,000 feet above the floor of the jungle,
was an extinct volcano. A conscientious prospector could sift
the alluvial grades up at the ridge and eke out an existence.
The outbreak of the war in 1939 did little to affect the way of
life in the Solomons. It was at this time that Australia organized the nucleus of the coastwatcher movement there. The
group was composed of men in their middle years, jungle-

hardened and experienced in dealing with the natives. One of them wrote to a friend in Sydney:

"If the Nips come, they'll only find rain and a pile of empties. I'll be off fighting with my cobbers."

The man who wrote this note was eighty years old.

The Japs came eventually and their coming was down from the north, by way of New Britain. There was no mass hysteria, no exodus, and certainly no confusion. In three years' time their hopes of expansion had succeeded to the point where they were occupying the Shortlands and Buka Passage; and, shortly after, Buin. But with the occupation of Rabaul, the Japanese had achieved striking distance for their long-range bombers, and now it was time to sight on the Solomons.

The first enemy flights roared down the island chain in March, and the wily Australians moved their radio station to the neighboring island of Tanambogo. They left a dummy antenna mast for the Japanese to bomb, however, and this the enemy did with unfaltering precision. As Japanese bombs became more and more frequent, the coastwatcher movement grew. These men had only portable teleradios and loyal natives to assist them in their spying operation; but their network, which kept in constant touch with Sydney, was considered first rate.

As the pace of the bombings accelerated in the late spring, the resident commissioner packed up his important papers, picked up his rifle, and began fighting back. Bombings came twice a day, and on May 1 Tulagi was subjected to a particularly disastrous raid. The Australian Air Force lost its last flying boat at this time and the commissioner, hearing of the catastrophe, figured it was time for even the bravest man to get off Tulagi. So the island was abandoned as the Japanese prepared to launch their invasion.

At Rabaul, the newly-acquired Japanese naval base to the north, large-scale operations were about to begin. Airfields were under construction and transports and cargo ships were bringing in men and supplies from other theaters of war. These were crack detachments of the Kure Marines, the best amphibious fighters of the Imperial Navy. Seventeenth Army was ferrying in planes and more troops. The Eighth Fleet had been reactivated and a new Commander Outer South Seas Force was due to arrive. A two-star admiral, who would see action at Coral Sea, came down from Truk with eleven ships and a number of construction men. Inasmuch as they would be leaving soon anyway, and since liberty at Rabaul was bad, few went ashore. A convoy was forming up at Simpson Harbor, and most of the men guessed they would soon be going south.

CHAPTER 2

TOUGH, TIGHT-LIPPED Rear Admiral Kiyohide Shima, commander of the Tulagi invasion force, received a readiness report at his headquarters on Rabaul two days later. He broke his red-and-white-striped battle flag on the cruiser-minelayer *Okinoshima,* and led eleven motley warships down The Slot. As the force passed the island of Santa Isabelle, an intrepid coastwatcher tapped out a message on his teleradio:

"Urgent! Enemy ships passing Thousand Ships Bay!"

It was the third of May, clear and pleasantly cool in the Solomons. A few coastwatchers at Tulagi had stoutly refused to be evacuated, believing they could get off the island at any time. Nobody was of the opinion that the Japanese ships would come so soon, and when the coastwatcher's message was received hasty steps were taken to assure that nothing of value would fall into Shima's hands.

The coming of the Japanese Co-Prosperity Sphere was reported several times as the ships moved leisurely to the south. But by now the original message had been transmitted to MacArthur's headquarters in Australia, and plans to thwart the southern move were already under way. Task Force 17 was patrolling along the edges of the Coral Sea, looking for trouble. And it had the pilots, bombs and planes to give plenty of punishment.

Nevertheless, the Japanese juggernaut was in motion and Admiral Shima sailed unopposed into Tulagi Roads. He gave the orders to drop anchor and put ashore the landing force. No shot rang out from the beach.

Shima's force consisted of a machine-gun company, two anti-tank gun platoons, and a number of laborers, divided into two groups. Lieutenant Juntaro Maruyama was put in command of the Tulagi detachment, while a second group under Lieutenant Kakichi Yashimoto was landed on Gavutu.

Shima paced his flag bridge, a happy man. The entire operation had been so simple, so uncluttered. He had virtually walked in unopposed and taken over the lower Solomons for the Emperor. Where Japan's forces trod, there was never opposition. He thought back to the time of the Woosung landing, five years before—an easy job, that one! His mind spun quickly over the landing at Malay, Singapore, and the Netherlands East Indies. Always, it seemed to the admiral, it was the same for Japan's amphibious forces.

Shima was proud to lead this little task force toward bigger and better goals. He was pleased to be a part of the inner workings. But he was dead wrong about the ease with which the Solomons would be occupied.

"With the cooperation of the South Seas Army Detachment and the Navy," Japanese planners wrote, "we will occupy Port Moresby and important positions on Tulagi and in south-eastern New Guinea. We will establish air bases and strengthen our air operations in the Australian area." This was the gist of Japan's Operation MO.

Imperial armed forces had powerful ambitions and, in the light of past events, there was no reason to question the reasonableness of their aspirations. Port Moresby, the key to Papua, was the stepping stone to New Guinea and the launching pad for Japanese bombers and warships striking that lifeline of communications, Australia. Japan wanted Port Moresby—wanted it badly enough to seize small clusters of islands in that area, thus making available various gateways to this valuable arena from which they could devitalize Australia.

There were complications, however. Knowing that the United States had about 200 long-range bombers—some of which had made reconnaissance flights as far north as New Ireland—at Australian airfields, Japan feared a large-scale operation. Unquestionably, if ships were used, they would be seen by reconnaissance planes and reported to the Allies in sufficient time to allow for a mass strike. Perhaps the entire Operation MO would be lost, Japanese planners thought. Therefore, they would come down to the south in slow stages, a few ships at a time.

Admiral Shima appeared on the scene at this time. Inasmuch as Japan was readying the Midway strike, no great force could be spared and Shima's ships were necessarily a composite group. Even if they were lost during the step-by-step move to the south, the loss would not be prohibitive. But Rear Admiral Tadaichi Hara's carriers *Shokaku* and *Zuikaku* and a number of cruisers were around in the Coral Sea, and these would provide a striking force for Shima's miniscule operation. Tulagi was merely a part of the Moresby operation and Shima was just another cog in the wheel.

The Imperial schedule included the occupation of this island on May 4. This meant that the communication lifeline would be cut and Japan would have successfully blocked off the Solomons. The Port Moresby invasion group would then depart from Rabaul on the following day and, by May 10, land amphibious forces at the objective. Intricate Japanese planning was based on the supposition that the United States carriers would follow the enemy into the Coral Sea, whereupon Japanese forces were to close in and annihilate them. As were *all* Japanese plans, Operation MO was well conceived but shortsighted, and it didn't take Admiral Nimitz very long to figure out the next move on the naval chessboard.

Admiral Nimitz alerted MacArthur, with the result that about 300 Army and Royal Australian planes were placed at strategic airfields in Australia. Nimitz could muster only about 150 planes from the carriers *Yorktown* and *Lexington*. He cajoled the Australians into giving a few ships and commanders, and these, together with the few warships already stationed there (MacArthur's Navy, it was called) were warned to stand by for invasion.

Appraised of what was in the wind, the plucky Australians around Tulagi held their breaths.

Admiral Shima's occupation force appeared on the button—May 4—and began a placid unloading. But Shima didn't conceive of the nefarious things which Nimitz and MacArthur had dreamed up for his reception! After all, there were only a handful of ships and a green island at the former Royal Australian flying-boat station when Shima dropped chain.

The Japanese admiral had no notion that his every movement was under observation by the Australian cloak-and-dagger operatives. He also had no notion that his course down The Slot had been observed and duly reported, or that coastwatchers had radioed Sydney that the Japanese occupation force had "dropped the hook" in Tulagi Roads. Shima, whose particular obsession was detail, took station on the wingtip of the cruiser-minelayer *Okinoshima* and directed the unessential job of arranging the line-up of his ships. It was getting dark, and the admiral was in a hurry to finish the chore and move on.

Many hundreds of miles from this tranquil scene, Rear Admiral Frank Jack Fletcher, fifty-nine, commanding Task Force 17 aboard the *Yorktown,* received the report that the Solomons were in the process of being occupied. The *Yorktown* and *Lexington* traveled together but were actually miles apart, because the latter was fueling her destroyers. When the message was brought to the bridge, Admiral Fletcher—an easy going, affable sort who never rushed into anything—was fueling his own destroyers. He ordered that fuel lines be disconnected as soon as possible. Fletcher's standing orders were to destroy enemy ships, shipping, or aircraft whenever and wherever found.

"Let's get going. I've been waiting months for a crack at those jokers—free up those fueling lines!" Fletcher snapped.

"But what about our other forces?" his chief-of-staff asked.

Fletcher's reply was characteristic. "Let's not wait for anything. Let's get 'em!"

The American admiral then curtly ordered the shaping of a new course that would put his planes within striking distance of Tulagi, and barreled off at 24 knots. It was the beginning of a very long night aboard the *Yorktown,* on the bridge where Fletcher was poring over the charts and in the ready room where the pilots received their first briefing. The big question uppermost in everybody's mind was: would the Japs still be there for the strike?

They were—and still in the precise unloading formation which Admiral Shima had ordered.

At 6:30 the following morning, with the wind gusting out of the north and the seas running high, the *Yorktown* turned into the wind to launch her strike. The attack was composed of twelve TBD (Devastators), torpedo planes, and 28 SBD (Dauntless Dive Bombers). Fletcher ordered a Combat Air Patrol of six F4F-3 (Wildcats) to provide an umbrella.

"Send 'em up!" Fletcher barked, and a few moments later a steady succession of planes thundered across the carrier's flight deck. The admiral watched the parade until the last plane had disappeared.

While Fletcher was commuting between the ready room to "see if there was anything coming over the damned radio" and the bridge, the strike moved down on the Solomons. Here the weather was clear, hot and windless. The eleven Japanese ships were lying at anchor and their crews were on a stand-by condition, with all guns unmanned. Shima himself was in his sea cabin reading a Tokyo newspaper which had been flown down to Rabaul.

The roar of aircraft filled the admiral's ears. Shima ran to the bridge tip to see what was happening. The American attack was coming in from the south. Excitedly, Shima called out a string of orders, while sirens screamed and crews frantically worked to get under way. The sound of the admiral's voice was lost in a welter of explosions as bombers peeled off and dove on the helpless ships.

"Attack! Attack! There they are below us!" The voice of Lieutenant Bill Short boomed suddenly over the *Yorktown's* radio. The sound of exploding bombs and now numerous bits of refreshing dialogue drifted over the airwaves. Frank Jack Fletcher sat back, lit a cigarette, and vicariously enjoyed the mauling his planes were giving the Imperial Navy. He glanced at his watch: 8:15 A.M. He had all day and no place to go. Somebody poured the admiral a cup of coffee, and he said: "It's just like listening to the fights!"

For Shima, however, it was a fight for survival. *Okinoshima's* anti-aircraft batteries put up a lively scrap. The stench of cordite and the hiccoughing of guns blended in a smoky, raucous cacophony. All the ships of the force were sending up red-and-white spirals of flame. Tongues of livid yellow fire danced higher than the bridge of the destroyer *Kikuzuki*, as she took a thousand-pound bomb amidships and heeled over.

Geysers of black water lofted hundreds of feet into the air, and in the midst of this turmoil desperate men maneuvered their ships in a ballet of death. American planes, buzzing like angry hornets, screamed down and punched a mighty hole in Savo Sound—a hole caused by the loosing of 28,000 pounds of explosive.

Next, the torpedo planes roared into the fray, skimming low over the water, directly into the teeth of the enemy's anti-aircraft fire, disgorging at will under the order to fire independently the "fish" they carried in their distended bellies. Japanese gunners were not equal to this onslaught and the minesweeper *Tama Maru* showed canted decks to the planes as two bombs detonated on her port and starboard, evenly distanced athwartships.

Shima's cruiser-minelayer was to survive by radical maneuvering in this maelstrom of steel and fire, but only seven days later American bombs would fall more accurately and she would slip beneath the waves. All day the carrier pilots came back to their targets. Shima, who had grown hoarse screaming over the radio for help from his own carriers— were too far away to help—fought the "Battle of Tulagi!" by himself.

Japanese gunners managed to down several carrier planes, the pilots and crews of which were soon succored by Australian coastwatchers. These men bore witness to the wild chase of the destroyer *Yuzuki*, which was under strafing fire from four Navy planes. This fire killed her skipper and bridge crew, and the tin can then "ran herself until after steerage could take over." Admiral Fletcher went back to his bridge.

(At 4:43 P.M. the *Yorktown* called it quits and took aboard the last strikes, departing the area before the Japs could turn around and destroy her. The Coral Sea into which the *Yorktown* sailed with the ill-fated *Lexington*, consorts and oilers, was to open new vistas for Navy pilots. Eluding the complicated enemy trap, the Navy dispatched the ʾrrier *Shoho* and put two somewhat first-line carriers out of commission for months. United States losses were about the same as the Japanese—even slightly less, all things considered—but a great moral victory had been won. The threatened invasion of Port Moresby was scrapped.)

On the island of Savo, a coastwatcher saw the entire battle from a perch high atop a palm tree, and his reports, described as "most accurate and colorful," were passed on to the authorities in Sydney.

A troubled calm descended on the Solomon Islands, and lasted for about two weeks. Coastwatchers who were trapped in the area, stayed where they were and prayed for invasion. They realized that it was only a matter of time before Japanese patrols caught them. Nevertheless, they continued to feed pertinent bits of imformation to Australia:

"The Japanese reinforced Tulagi, Tanambogo and Gavutu, working day and night to strengthen these islands," wrote coastwatcher Feldt. "A flying-boat base was established in the harbor, the aircraft ranging over the surrounding seas on daily reconnaissance flights."

From Gold Ridge, 4,000 feet up on Guadalcanal's slopes, a coastwatcher reported: "Every time I look there are enemy ships arriving at Tulagi with supplies."

These heroic few struggled alone, holding fast to the belief that eventually help would come. But only Japanese patrols came, further depleting their ranks. Allied stock was at a low ebb these days, and it was to get lower yet before the light of invasion finally glimmered on these miserable islands.

CHAPTER 3

CHURCHILL, REVIEWING the war, asked what were American intentions regarding the Pacific theater. Specifically he asked if the United States could "offer New Zealand and Australia each the support of an American division" (to replace troops already fighting in the Middle East) . . . and recommended that "plans be made to prepare an expeditionary force on the United States West Coast for attacks on the Japanese in 1943."

To both the question and recommendation, President Roosevelt replied in the affirmative. It was at this time that Admiral King wrote a memorandum to the president saying, "We cannot let Australia and New Zealand down. They are our brothers, and we must not allow them to be overrun by Japan."

Roosevelt added his own floral piece in a cable to Churchill: "There is no use in giving a further single thought to Singapore or to the Dutch Indies. They are gone. Australia must be held, and we are willing to undertake that."

Accordingly, with pomp and fanfare, an offensive operation came into being. Called Operation Watchtower, it was not to be mounted for a year. During this period the United States would have sufficient time to plan. There were many things Admiral King had in mind for the Navy, and he was not loath to speak out in a loud, unquavering voice. Only a couple of months before, he had written to the Honorable Carl Vinson, Chairman of the Committee on Naval Affairs:

> ". . . I feel that I can say to you that 1942 seems to me to be the critical year for our cause. We must turn out every plane and ship and accompanying munitions that the present productive capacity is capable of. In my opinion, every existing means of war production should be brought up to a twenty-four hour basis before any materials, labor or

22

management are made available for expansion. In other words, only those things should be applied to expansion which cannot be applied to bring our existing production up to a twenty-four hour basis."

Now that the future had been clearly presaged, Admiral King, in a letter to Rear Admiral C. S. Freeman, Commandant of the Thirteenth Naval District, again expressed himself:

"The plain facts of the matter are that we have not the 'tools' wherewith to meet the enemy at all the points he is threatening—Hawaii *must* be held —we must do what we can to maintain the line of communications with Australia—you know how little 'left over' for yourself and Greenslade. (Freeman was in Seattle; Rear Admiral Greenslade in San Francisco.) The submarine situation on the east coast approaches the 'desperate.' All in all, we have to do the best with what we've got."

The country was tooling up, the factory workers responding with enthusiasm to the needs (doubletime for overtime, and work a six-day week if you will) of the services.

The Joint Chiefs had met again, designating General Mac-Arthur as Supreme Commander Allied Forces. MacArthur, who was to be headquartered in Australia, held sway over the "Philippines, Australia, and all the waters between them; the whole of New Guinea and all of the Bismarck and Solomon Islands."

Admiral Nimitz, in addition to his Pacific Fleet command, was given the additional job of CINCPOA (Commander-in-Chief Pacific Ocean Area), with the North, Central and South Pacific Areas falling into his command.

Vice Admiral Robert L. Ghormley, an energetic and capable naval operations planner, came on the scene from London the day before the Doolittle raid on Tokyo, April 17. Ghormley had been in London as Special Naval Observer, but the arrival there of Admiral Stark made his presence no longer necessary. Besides, Admiral Nimitz was shopping around for a good man in this vast area he'd suddenly acquired.

Ghormley was tagged.

Admiral King greeted him in his office, gave Ghormley barely enough time to catch his breath, and told him of the

Joint Chief's division of things and of the Navy's new South
Pacific Force and Area. He said:

> "You have a large and important area and a
> most difficult task. I do not have the tools to give
> you to carry out that task as it should be done.
> You will establish your headquarters in Auckland
> with an advanced base at Tongatabu. In time,
> possibly this fall, we hope to start an offensive
> from the South Pacific."

For Admiral King, a man of precious few words, this was
a long speech. For Ghormley, it was a challenge which would
turn out to be a bomb. He accepted the orders eagerly and
thereupon set out for the next two weeks to collect a staff. A
lot of admirals were in Washington at the time, but a lot of
good ones weren't. Ghormley, however, was a good shopper
and he came up with some 40 junior and two flag rank officers,
Rear Admiral Daniel "Uncle Dan" Callaghan and Brigadier
General Dewitt Peck, USMC. Both men were only too well
aware of the fact that these billets were hot. Exactly *how* hot,
they were not to learn till later.

To Callaghan and Peck fell the difficult task of finding
charts of the Solomons. The only ones they were able to come
up with were Admiralty editions of 1897 and German editions
of 1908. This, to say the least, made the planned operation all
the more troublesome.

The vice admiral had an interesting time in Washington.
Under the impression that his assignment was a newly conceived affair, Ghormley suddenly learned that the War and
Navy Departments had been on the project for three months
and that they had been having tough sledding. Logistically
speaking, getting the necessary men and machines to Australia was difficult if not nearly impossible at times. They
had to be secured from everywhere and anywhere.

"Admiral King," Morison states, "was so disturbed by the
delay in (advance) base construction that he appointed Rear
Admiral Richard E. Byrd, the Antarctic explorer, and repre-
sentatives of all Navy Department bureaus concerned with
logistics, to inspect the sites and make recommendations."

Two years later, Admiral King, in a memorandum to the
Secretary of the Navy, was to summarize the Pacific war as
being in four stages:

"(a) The defensive, when we were engaged almost exclusively in protecting our shores and our lines of communication from the encroachment of the enemy.

"(b) The defensive-offensive, during which although our operations were chiefly defensive in character, we were able nevertheless to take certain offensive measures.

"(c) The offensive-defensive, covering the period immediately following the seizure of the initiative, but during which we still had to use a large part of our forces to defend our recent gains.

"(d) The offensive, which was when our advance bases were no longer seriously threatened and we became able to attack the enemy at places of our own choosing."

The United States was then only on the offensive-defensive, and Vice Admiral Ghormley, to whom all this trouble had fallen, tried his utmost to get things going. After about a week in wartime Washington, the admiral was happy to gather his staff and their sundry problems and journey to Pearl Harbor for another series of conferences with Admiral Nimitz. His job was monumental, and it had to be done on a shoestring. And, of course, unequivocal success was expected. Admiral Ghormley had some catastrophic headaches these days, and the kindly Admiral Nimitz couldn't be of much help other than to supply him with a crackerjack carrier officer, Rear Admiral John J. McCain, who was to serve as Commander Aircraft South Pacific Area.

McCain took over fast. Within a week he was off to Noumea in the Fijis and his two-star flag was flying from the *Tangier*. Now the plan situation for the area, at least, was under control. Ghormley, meeting him there a few days later, found himself confronted with an unusual, unexpected, and tense political situation. The French islands of the Pacific, excepting Wallis, had swung to General De Gaulle. One of De Gualle's admirals, D'Argenlieu, the commissioner, had already been the victor in a political embroglio which threatened to have serious repercussions. Many people of the islands were pro-Axis, the ousted man had friends, and a blow-up was in the wind when Ghormley met Contre-admiral d'Argenlieu that first morning. But Ghormley was capable of soothing ruffled feathers.

Long years of diplomacy had given him a certain touch—

a flair, as it were—for the right words at the right time. Ghormley now used such words on the French admiral, the admiral's opponent, the forces of the Free French and even on the pro-Axis element. To the French admiral Ghormley assigned a mission: the openly hostile island of Wallis was to be taken over by the Free French. D'Argenlieu warmed to this job. He planted the French flag aboard a French corvette and steamed for Wallis on the morning of May 26. Within hours, the island fell. Ghormley, with the political situation now under control, was free to move Marines and Seabees to Wallis the next day. Next he turned his attention to the Army.

Major General A. M. Patch was present with his Americal Division (America-Caledonia). Here Ghormley met with the warmest cooperation and assistance in setting up the advance bases he required. Although the United States was short of everything, particularly the heavy equipment needed by the Seabees, somehow the job was done. By and large, it was done with the help of the Army, frequently with an assidious avoidance of red tape. The advance-base problem was met, and the headquarters of Operation Watchtower was now Espiritu Santu in the Hebrides.

Historic events which would shape the course of the war were in the making.

In Japan, the Midway sortie was being planned, and Admiral Nimitz, who understood the alarming lay of things (the Japanese code had been broken and, unknown to them, the U.S. Navy was intercepting all their messages), suggested to General MacArthur that the time to advance Operation Watchtower—the offensive—was now. McArthur vetoed the suggestion as not being feasible. In fact, MacArthur frequently disagreed with Nimitz, so that their disputes had to be referred to Washington. The decision handed down by the Joint Chiefs as a result of the squabble was, in effect, that the Santa Cruz Islands, Tulagi and adjacent positions would be Admiral Nimitz' province, while Guadalcanal and the waters to the west would be MacArthur's.

Ghormley, at this time a much beset man, moved his flag to the USS *Rigel* in Auckland Harbor, New Zealand, at the end of May, believing that Operation Watchtower was progressing at a normal rate of speed. But the events of the succeeding few days would very much change his mind.

It was now June, and at Midway a great battle had been fought between carrier forces, the United States Navy clearly emerging as the victor. In Washington, Admiral King was beating the war drum. The offensive should be taken immediately! Hit 'em hard, now! Hit 'em while they're still groggy! MacArthur wanted to hit Rabaul. Nimitz was advancing the Solomons idea. Each had a point.

MacArthur asked for naval forces, including two carriers, to carry out his plans. Admiral King was adamant in the negative reply he sent back. MacArthur correspondingly vetoed Nimitz' plan. Then the Joint Chiefs again stepped in. On June 25, while Ghormley was under the impression that he still had plenty of time, a directive came down from King that an offensive be launched immediately against the enemy forces in the lower Solomons. Target date was set for August 1. Admiral Nimitz was the bearer of these happy tidings.

These were days of dissension for Ernest J. King and George C. Marshall, the latter responding positively to the idea that an invasion be launched as quickly as possible, but negatively to the proposition that a navy man be in charge of the show.

"The whole Pacific is involved," Marshall said firmly. Whereupon, he went on to point out why the logical commander was MacArthur.

Meanwhile, Admiral Ghormley, a dispirited and frustrated soul, was told that the 1st Marine Division under Major General Alexander J. Vandergrift was enroute. Twenty-thousand Marines were to be available. During these days Ghormley was to acquire the services of other capable men: Vice Admiral Frank Jack Fletcher, who had gotten his third star after the Coral Sea and Midway battles; Rear Admiral Richard K. Turner, the tough, grizzled commander of Watchtower's transport divisions; and, of course, there was Rear Admiral John S. McCain. All in all, Ghormley's lot at this juncture could have been worse.

But on June 25th the boom was lowered from an unexpected source. A message was received at Pearl Harbor that a reconnaissance plane had observed the Japanese building an airstrip at Guadalcanal—a strip which, if made operational, could cost the Allies the Pacific. It could very well mean another Japanese offensive. That was all that King needed to hear.

Again he went to the Joint Chiefs. The decision came down quickly. Nimitz would assume command, with General MacArthur in support, until Tulagi was secured. Once secured, command would pass to the general, who "would coordinate a move up the Solomons to Salamau and Lae." The two would then converge on Rabaul, which was rapidly becoming the Japanese staging area in the South Pacific. D-Day was set for August 7.

CHAPTER 4

ADMIRAL GHORMLEY, who would come off in this affair as badly as anyone yet alive when Savo passed into history, was the first to command a naval expeditionary force since 1898.

Although he tried hard to look on the bright side during these chaotic days, there seemed to be no bright side except that Admirals King and Nimitz were squarely behind him. This was of little consolation. Callaghan, the fatherly senior partner of the Ghormley firm, was to remark a few days before his death, "He worried about everything, and I can't say that I blame him."

Ghormley, now squarely on the hook to produce an amphibious invasion in the Solomon Islands, did his best. On July 17 he submitted and had approved the Operational Plan of Watchtower. It was a good plan, and it employed the talents of excellent men who knew their craft. His organization was divided into three main forces:

The Carrier Force (Task Force 61), Rear Admiral Leigh Noyes commanding, was composed of three elements from Nimitz' domain—11, 16, and 18. It included three carriers —*Saratoga, Enterprise* and *Wasp*—the new battleship *North Carolina*, five heavy cruisers, an anti-aircraft cruiser, and sixteen destroyers.

The Amphibious Force (Task Force 62), Rear Admiral Richmond K. Turner commanding, included the Fleet Marine Force, two light cruisers, six heavy cruisers, thirteen attack transports, fifteen destroyers, four destroyer transports and five mine-sweepers.

The Shore-Based Aircraft (Task Force 63), Rear Admiral John S. McCain commanding, included all aircraft in the operational area except those of the aircraft carriers.

In tactical command aboard was the now Vice Admiral Frank Jack Fletcher, who was to fly his bunting from the yard of *Saratoga*. Fletcher, remarked Major John Zimmerman, writing for the Marine Corps, was already well known to the

29

corps for his attempt to relieve Wake Island. He was well known by the same token, to the Navy's carrier pilots for take-charge tactics at Coral Sea and Midway.

"Just knowing that Fletcher was going to be around was great for morale," said a division commander of the expedition.

At this time Ghormley passed the word that dress rehearsals were in order, and he prepared to shift his three-starred flag from New Zealand to Noumea to exercise strategic command. Now the stage was set. All disputes over jurisdiction had been settled and the target was well fixed in the minds of everyone concerned. Into Ghormley's command passed the Anzac cruiser and destroyer flotilla under Rear Admiral V. A. C. Crutchley, former skipper of H.M.S. *Warspite,* who was to serve as gun support to Turner and that admiral's second-in-command.

The Marines, meanwhile, were at Wellington, New Zealand, with their seabags packed and their battle equipment ready. The only detail that concerned Vandergrift was not knowing "too damned much" about the objective. Nor did anybody, as a matter of fact. A number of reconnaissance flights over the area were made and aerial photographs taken. This proved exactly nothing other than the fact that the enemy was occupied in building airfields on Guadalcanal, which everybody knew anyway.

Reflecting on these troubled times, Major Zimmerman records a letter from Colonel E. F. Kumpe, Engineer Corps, to Dr. John Miller, an Army historian and former Marine, written in 1948:

"The rush job at that time was the preparation of photomaps for Guadalcanal. The photography was flown by Colonel Karl Polifka of the Air Force . . . and consisted of two strips along the northern shore of the island. The following information is not a tale of woe, but a very distressing account of what eventuated at that time. The photographs were printed in the north, and the prints and negatives assigned A-1 priority for shipment to GHQ and subsequently to the map plant. They were diverted for approximately ten days, due to a whim of the transportation officer at Townsville, and subsequently delivered to the map plant. Unfortunately, I do not recall the specific date, but it was in advance of the operation.

"No bulk distribution request was received and it was a matter of considerable surprise (to say the least) to discover that neither the photographs nor the photomaps had been available to the 1st Marine Division. An informal investigation after the operation brought out the information that the maps had been lost in the tremendous pile of boxes incident to the organizing of the base establishment of South Pacific (SOPAC). On subsequent occasions some oblique photographs captured from the Japanese were the only sources of maps during the opening phases of the operation."

In retrospect, these pathetically humorous accounts serve well to explain a terse comment by a member of this command: "If I'd been the admiral, I'd have turned in my uniform and gone home!"

Ghormley did not. The planners buckled down to the impossible job, securing their information wherever possible. It was the unhappy lot of Colonel Frank Goettge, intelligence officer of the 1st Marine Division, to locate anybody from the Solomon Islands—planters, miners, coastal traders, former coastwatchers living in Australia and New Zealand—and persuade them to impart whatever information they had. Goettge rounded up a few people who offered a few vague answers.

Although in most instances these intelligence sources could not speak specifically, they did tell something coherent about Tulagi and Guadalcanal. It helped. The islands were physically dissimilar. Tulagi, relatively small, was heavily wooded, with rough terrain—very little of it level ground. Its chief importance, of course, was its unusually good harbor facilities. Two small, hilly islands, Tanambogo and Gavutu—where the British had set up their radio—lay to the east.

Guadalcanal, already described, was 20 miles across Sealark Channel. Malaria and rainfall were its chief characteristics. There was little information to go on, but it was better than nothing. The Marines knew, for instance, that there were a number of rivers on Guadalcanal, which could be forded at certain times. They knew, too, that both Tulagi and Guadalcanal offered treacherous shore lines because of coral formations, and it was really this knowledge that decided them on Lunga (Guadalcanal), with its fairly good access, as the point of departure.

As to the enemy's movements, strength and fortifications, the information forthcoming and already on hand from the coastwatchers was enough. Japanese headquarters was at Tulagi, but the enemy also had installations on Gavutu and

Tanambogo, and were constructing the strip on Guadalcanal. About 8,000 troops were supposed to be present in the islands. Actually, including construction troops, who doubled in brass as soldiers when needed, there were only about 2,000 men.

Ghormley left the other details to Vandergrift. The latter promptly assigned General William H. Rupertus, assistant division commander, to command the Tulagi force. This included the 1st Marine Raider Battalion (Lieut. Col. Merrit A. Edson); the 1st Parachute Battalion (Major Robert H. Williams); and the 2nd Battalion, 5th Marines (Lieut. Col. Harold E. Rosecrans). The Marines assigned to this landing were the best trained and therefore considered the sharpest.

Vandergrift, with two Marine battalions, was to land at Guadalcanal. Aotea Quay, at Wellington, New Zealand, was the Marine staging area, and a frenetic area it was. There were labor troubles with stevedores, meager dockside facilities, inadequate food supplies, and perishables that perished. In addition, transports which were supposed to be there weren't, until the last minute.

"During the mounting out, certain modifications of the logistic plan had become necessary," Major Zimmerman says. "As finally loaded, the Marine force was carrying sixty days' supplies, ten units of fire for all weapons, the minimum individual baggage ... actually required to live and to fight."

Despite these handicaps, on the bright and sunny morning of July 22 the Marines, escorted by the cruisers of Admiral Turner's Task Force 62, got under way for dress rehearsals. Turner's flag was aboard the *McCawley*. His forces would come from a number of widely separated points before final departure. The massive convoy was forming and, 400 miles south of the Fijis, the beset Ghormley thought to give a moment to the problems of his subordinates. Accordingly, on July 26 he ordered a rendezvous aboard the aircraft carrier *Saratoga*, where his commanders then met to iron out their differences.

"Everybody deplored the lack of time to plan carefully and thoroughly, but saw no way out except to whip plans into shape as rapidly as possible," Zimmerman concluded.

For the next three days, rehearsals were held in the Fijis— crude and costly rehearsals which prompted Vandergrift to exclaim in disgust that "they were a complete bust!"

A Coast Guard coxwain was equally vociferous: "It was a holy mess that just about cost me my boat."

Rehearsals completed, the Amphibious Force, screened by a

warship escort, got under way for the Solomons. Aboard the
transport *Crescent City,* correspondent Richard Tregaskis
found Marines in good humor after the hullaballoo at the
staging areas. "Chattanooga Choo-Choo" and pin-ups were
the order of the day. Father Francis W. Kelly, who had come
to the corps by way of a Pennsylvania mining town, held
church services that first Sunday at sea. The services were conducted in a messhall—the first shift for Catholics, the second
for Protestants. The subject of Father Kelly's sermon was
duty, "and was obviously pointed toward our coming landing
somewhere in Japanese-held territory."

There were moments of relaxation when a gyrene could
get candy (porgy bait) at the ship's service, and moments of
a more studious nature. There were classes in tactics and
fighting, and instructions from a former copra plantation
owner on the rivers of Guadalcanal. Memorandums were
posted in quarters, a typical example being one which described the infamous Tenaru:

> ". . . The river follows a serpentine course with a
> current averaging four knots. During the rainy sea-
> son and flood the water rushes at much greater speed.
> The river is full of deep holes and well over a man's
> head. . . ."

Splendid reading material! The Marines took it all in stride.
On D-Day minus three, a mimeographed message was posted
on every ship in the force:

> "On August 7 we will recapture Tulagi and
> Guadalcanal Islands which are now in the hands of
> the enemy. In this first forward step toward clearing
> the Japanese out of conquered territory we have
> strong support from the Pacific Fleet and from the
> air, surface and submarine forces in the South Pacific
> and Australia. It is significant of victory that we see
> here shoulder to shoulder the United States Navy, .
> Marines and Army, and the Australian and New Zea-
> land Air, Naval and Army services. I have confidence
> that all elements of this armada will in skill and cour-
> age show themselves fit comrades of those brave men
> who already have dealt the enemy mighty blows for
> our great cause. God bless you all! R. K. Turner."

Aboard a transport a group of Marines was observed scaling
half dollars across the surface of the ocean. Asked about this,

one of the men shrugged and said, "Where we're going, who the hell needs money?" Outwardly there was no fear. The men were calm and, as the voyage was nearing its end, reflective:

"I checked my notes over and over again to see if I had done everything that I thought needed to be done," a Marine major said. He was to lead his company ashore at Tulagi. "I had collected the last letters that the boys had written and were leaving aboard the ship, because many of us felt that possibly we wouldn't get a chance to write letters again, maybe never."

The last night of the voyage was clear, and the sea was calm. On deck, there was the sibilant hiss of the bow wave falling away, and some phosphorescence to fire the water. There were thoughts of submarine attacks, but no submarines came. A quartering moon shone dully over the ships steaming in long lanes, the escorts riding herd on the flanks and ahead. In the sleeping quarters where Marines lay in three-tiered bunks, few slept. At ten minutes before three the task force split into two groups, one moving toward the distant outline of Guadalcanal, silhouetted in black, ahead; the other moving toward the farther outline of Savo Island. Behind it was Tulagi.

No one on deck could tear his eyes from these landfalls. Throughout the force there was one thought: Will the surprise be complete? It was. False dawn streaked in the heavens and not long after, it seemed, it was gray light and 5:30. Aboard the carriers *Enterprise, Wasp* and *Saratoga* planes were roaring off flight decks to be over the objectives when the bombardment opened. On the transports, Marines checked their watches.

At 6:13 the guns of the *Quincy* roared out an 8-inch salvo off Lunga Point, Guadalacanal. *Astoria, Ellet, Quincy* and *Vincennes* triggered off mighty broadsides a moment later. Then the Navy bombers appeared, roaring down in unison and bombing the beaches. They spotted a lone schooner off the coast of Guadalcanal, and singled it out for a concerted strafing and bombing attack. Aboard the transports, Marines watched in awed silence, standing in full battle regalia at the railings as they waited for the signal to disembark.

All about the horizon there were deep orange flashes, and the roar of tremendous salvos leaving the guns of the warships. The shores of Guadalcanal and Tulagi erupted geysers of black earth far into the sky, and very quickly fires appeared along the Tulagi beaches. Now cargo nets were lowered from the transports and landing craft swung outboard on huge davits.

At 6:47, from the bridge of the *Neville,* Captain George B. Ashe, the lanky, taciturn commander of transport division Yoke, spat out fateful words into the intercom set: "Land the landing force!"

CHAPTER 5

AT RABAUL, 570 miles from the Allied invasion, the commander of the Japanese Eighth Fleet and the Outer South Seas Force was asleep in the ramshackle gray building which served as his headquarters ashore. This man was Rear Admiral Gunichi Mikawa, fifty-three, who had cut his teeth as Batdiv 3 under Admiral Chuichi Nagumo at Pearl Harbor and Midway.

Mikawa's Staff Communicator Captain Teraoka Hadai was the first to receive the bad news. Shocked and trembling with anger, Hadai rushed off to the admiral's quarters and awoke the commander of the Outer South Seas Force. Without a word the groggy Mikawa read the fateful message:

> "Tulagi under severe bombardment from the air and sea X Enemy task force sighted X One battleship, two carriers, three cruisers, fifteen destroyers, and thirty to forty transports X"

Mikawa's response was immediate. He bolted upright and snapped: "Wake the staff. Arrange for all charts and maps. Find out the disposition of our forces here and at Kavieng. Get Captain Ohmae (Toshikazau Ohmae) on his feet. I'll be there in a moment."

A soft-spoken intellectual and an officer of wide experience, the admiral was still smarting from the Midway defeat. He had privately longed for the chance to avenge the loss of four first-line carriers, *Akagi, Kaga, Hiryu* and *Soryu;* the heavy cruiser *Mikuma;* 250 planes and the cream of Japanese naval aviation. Even as he dressed and hurried to the messhall where his staff was gathered, Mikawa's alert mind was grappling with this possibility: Was a decisive night engagement with the enemy feasible?

Captain Hadai met him and proffered a second

36

message: "0630 Enemy effecting simultaneous landings at Tulagi and Guadalcanal X."

Mikawa winced. He hurried to the wall map, where staff personnel were circling the invasion area and computing distances. An officer of the 25th Air Flotilla was standing by. But the quick deployment of men and ships was Mikawa's most pressing problem, and he devoted all his energy to this end. The forces of the Eighth Fleet simply weren't enough.

At Rabaul were the light cruisers *Tenryu* and *Yubari,* and the destroyer *Yunagi.* The admiral gave orders to have these ships get up steam and prepare to get under way. At Kavieng, farther to the north, was Crudiv 6 and heavy cruiser *Chokai.* The four components of the cruiser division were the *Aoba, Kinugasa, Kako* and *Furutaka.* Two of these heavy cruisers were under way, and Mikawa promptly diverted them back to where they were needed urgently.

Submarine Squadron 7 was available for duty, and these five long-range I-boats were ordered to concentrate around the Guadalcanal area and attack American ships in the vicinity of the beachheads. The admiral, in addition, diverted destroyers *Tatsuta, Uzuki* and *Yuzuki* from convoy duty off Buna.

Submarines *RO-33* and *RO-34* were pulled off station in the Port Moresby-Australia grid.

The wheels were turning! Mikawa snapped out instructions to Captain Ohmae, a crack navigator, that would have him grabbing dividers, checking fuel capacities and calibrating time and distance. He wanted to arrive at Guadalcanal just about midnight, after a long day of sheer hell for the invader. Ohmae figured out a movement which would very nearly achieve this.

The admiral next turned his attention to the possibility of smashing the enemy carriers. To Commander Tadashi Nakajima of the 25th Air Flotilla he addressed an inquiry:

"How soon," he asked, "can you get some bombers and Zeros into the air?"

The usually confident Nakajima was flabbergasted. "We do not have many bombers, Admiral!" he replied. "The Zeroes have flown great distances in the past, sir, but I doubt if they can make a trip of nearly six hundred miles one way. Where will they land?"

"Buna," said Mikawa, tapping the map with his index finger. *"Anywhere."*

It was Mikawa's fervent hope that by sending up a flight and attacking the carriers off Guadalcanal, he could immobilize at least a part of the enemy. The warships, then, could do the rest. But this was merely wishful thinking on Mikawa's part, and he didn't bank too heavily on the accomplishments of the aircraft. There were only 78 planes at Rabaul, and after the last enemy air attack only a portion were in service.

It was now the moment that the light cruiser *San Juan,* off Guadalcanal, trained her guns on the small white building which was used as a Japanese radio station. In Mikawa's headquarters the staff communicator picked up the last message to be delivered by the Tulagi garrison. Mikawa read it in silence. The time was 8:05. His jaw muscles flickered, but he said nothing. The message read:

> "The enemy force is overwhelming X We will defend our positions to the death X"

The guns of the American cruiser roared and a salvo was on its way. In a few seconds the building and its occupants would cease to exist.

Mikawa said a silent prayer for the trapped men, then quickly busied himself in affairs of logistics. Meanwhile, Commander Nakajima returned to his headquarters. The 25th Flotilla's airmen were standing by. The reaction of the fighter pilots was as his had been, and the identical questions of these exasperated men filled the air. Nakajima brushed objections aside. By 8:30 a flight of 27 bombers, covered by Zero fighters, was winging toward Guadalcanal. He phoned his report to Mikawa.

The admiral bent his energies to the task of rounding up reinforcements for the beleaguered garrisons. He could muster a fairly respectable air strike, but getting troops was another matter.

He turned to the 17th Army ("Hyakutate's Force") representative, Colonel Shigeo Yano, asking if the Nankei Detachment were immediately available for further transfer to Guadalcanal. Here the interservice rivalry for which Japan was famed came into play. Yano's reply was that he was powerless to make a decision—that any decision would have to be made on Imperial General Headquarters level. This eliminated the Nankei Detachment, on which Mikawa had banked.

The admiral had no time to waste on recrimination. He turned his attention to the gathering of available forces and

Captain Masakiki Sakuma, a member of the staff, showed the admiral that it was possible to round up a few men anyway. These would serve some purpose, Sakuma told him. A reinforcement unit of 310 riflemen with several machine guns and roughly 100 men could be drawn from the Sasebo Special Naval Landing Force and the 81st Garrison Unit.

"Have them with full field equipment ready to leave at once," Mikawa responded. The *Meiyo Maru,* a transport, was available, as were the supply vessel *Soya* and the minelayer *Tsugaru,* which would serve as escorts. As details were being worked out, the heavy cruiser *Chokai* was ordered into Rabaul to embark Mikawa's staff, while Crudiv 6 headed for the rendezvous point in St. George Channel.

It was 10:30. Suddenly the morning was interrupted by unwelcome guests.

Overhead roared thirteen of General MacArthur's B-17's, on a bombing mission coordinated with the main landings at Guadalcanal and Tulagi. Led by Lt. Col. Richard H. Carmichael, sixteen planes had originally taken off that morning, refueled briefly at Port Moresby, and continued on again. Their mission was the Vunakanau airdrome at Rabaul.

One of the B-17's had crashed on takeoff, two had turned back because of engine trouble, but thirteen had completed the flight and were roaring over Mikawa's head. He had a profound sense of relief as he realized that the passing planes had singled out a different target than the waterfront. His cruisers were intact. At any rate, as a result of the American strike the admiral called a temporary halt of the staff meeting, and everyone went outside to watch the flight of the enemy bombers.

The B-17's made a shambles of the airfield and the bombers conviently parked there. One B-17 was shot down in flames by Zero fighters, while American gunners came home to claim seven Zeros.

Mikawa and his staff watched the show for a few minutes, then returned to the makeshift shore headquarters of the Eighth Fleet to attend to the myriad urgent details screaming for their attention.

(On Guadalcanal, 35 tons of five-inch ammo was falling— the hot gunnery of the men on the light cruiser *San Juan.*)

It was 10:45. Captain Ohmae called the admiral's attention to the fact that not many of the ships to be employed had ever operated together before. Mikawa realized this only too well. "Except for Crudiv 6 ships, they had never so much as trained together in steaming in column formation," Ohmae told him. Mikawa considered this problem, first giving orders to adjust course changes in night formation. Almost as if reassuring himself, he said:

"The commander of each ship is a skilled veteran. Maximum effectiveness can be achieved by a single-column formation."

Next Mikawa turned to the business of how to negotiate imperfectly charted seas and avoid the danger of underwater reefs. Acting at this juncture, on the advice of the commander of the 8th Base Force, Mikawa issued orders for charting a course southward through the central channel (The Slot), which was considered nearly deep enough to afford passage to a battleship.

The details of this plan were worked out by noon and forwarded to Tokyo for approval. Reaction wasn't long in coming.

"Dangerous and reckless!" Admiral Osami Nagano replied. For a few minutes he did nothing, but upon further consideration and consultation the Chief of the Naval General Staff reluctantly agreed to Mikawa's plan. At breakfast when the reply from Tokyo was communicated to him, Admiral Mikawa allowed himself to show his pleasure with a broad grin. He was thinking perhaps of the naval school which considered that warships were outmoded—in fact useless. The airplane was the coming thing, many officers contended. Build more carriers, they advocated, and the devil take capital ships!

Air power had come into its own since the Sino-Japanese war. The Imperial Navy enjoyed some unprecedented successes with the fly-boys. But to Gunichi Mikawa, still essentially a "battleship admiral" (as were other flag-rank officers) there was "nothing like a broadside fired into an enemy ship." In a sense, and a very real sense, this sort of thinking dominated the admiral's battle plan and his avid desire to eliminate any carriers in the area. Japan's gunners, second to none in night fighting, would now get a chance to prove their superiority during a pitch-black slugfest. Mikawa delighted in the prospect.

In Tokyo there were a few others who felt as he did about the use of gunships. For one, there was Rear Admiral Shigero Fukudome of the Naval General Staff who had written, "It is generally considered that the battleship is a worthy instrument of service when in the company of carriers. But until there are other means for nullifying the enemy's battleships, and planes alone cannot do it, our own battleship strength must be maintained."

Admiral Mikawa had practically committed these words to memory, and before too long he would make Shigero Fukudome look very good indeed.

Until 1 P.M., when the heavy cruiser *Chokai* entered Raboul Harbor, Admiral Mikawa and his staff worked out the details of the sortie. A second air-raid warning disrupted the meeting. False alarm. Mikawa's own aircraft were returning to Vunakanau airfield after a disappointing attempt to strike the enemy. None of the planes, the admiral heard, had sighted aircraft carriers, and there had been many losses.

"I watched the bombs curving in their long drop. Abruptly geysers of water erupted from the sea, but the enemy shipping sailed on undisturbed," a frustrated pilot reported to headquarters.

Mikawa listened to the report in silence. It only served to strengthen his resolve to sink the American shipping concentrated near Guadalcanal as soon as possible.

At 2:30, after clearing up last-minute details, Mikawa and his staff boarded the *Chokai*. Dock lines were hurriedly cast off and the gangway unshackled. Then the flagship, accompanied by light cruisers *Tenryu* and *Yubari*, with destroyer *Yunagi* racing ahead, moved past the shipping in Rabaul Harbor. At the yard of the 28-year-old cruiser was Mikawa's flag, bright and flapping vividly in the brassy midday light.

It was a fine day to be at sea, a fine feeling to have a ship beneath his feet again. Going out to the starboard wing, the admiral heard some of the staff discussing the coming battle. His mind spun across the waters to Setagaya, his home near Tokyo, to which he had returned after Midway and prior to reassignment to the Outer South Seas Force.

There had been only a few days at home, and most of that time was spent brooding about the Midway disaster. There, in his rock gardens, Mikawa had relived every phase of the carrier battle which cost Japan the initiative in the Pacific. Like others in command at Midway, defeat had left Admiral Mikawa stunned and bewildered, and groping for excuses.

An intellectual and a professional officer of wide experience, Mikawa's thoughts then, as now, were above all of his beloved homeland. If Japan had the opportunity to strike a blow, then nothing should be spared in an effort to make this blow a telling one. Perhaps, he thought, it might again lead to the Imperial Navy's superiority in the Pacific.

On the day of his appointment as Commander, Eighth Fleet, Captain Toshikazau Ohmae of his staff had visited the Mikawa home. The two men had talked over tea, Mikawa recalled now, after which Ohmae had departed with the admiral's instructions to look over the forward areas and then report back. At Truk, headquarters of Vice Admiral Shigeyoshi Inoue's Fourth Fleet, a staff member had told Ohmae of Japan's hopes for the So.omons. This area was relatively quiet, with no evidence of enemy feints. Mikawa had arrived at Rabaul, New Ireland, aboard the *Chokai,* escorted by Destroyer Division 9, on July 30, and had assumed command of the Outer South Seas Force from Inoue.

Admiral Mikawa set up headquarters in a ramshackle building, lacking window panes and toilet facilities, near the 2nd Air Group. Though a few of the necessities were reinstalled, the admiral seemed not to notice, either way. Concerned for the safety of his heavy cruisers, he had ordered them to the rear area of Kavieng so that they would be away from Allied bombers. It had been a farsighted precaution.

Mikawa remained standing on the bridge wing in silence. Three hours after ships had departed Rabaul there were lookout cries, indicating masts had been spotted. Soon the force would be a unit, and Mikawa put his binoculars on the silhouettes of *Aoba, Kako, Kinugasa* and *Furutaka.*

As these ships fell into line, the signal fluttered from the flag bridge: "Alert cruising disposition."

At dusk, Admiral Mikawa was fifteen miles off the coast of New Ireland, course north by east, and shaping to pass north of Buka at the head end of the Solomon Islands. It had been a long, hectic day, and Mikawa came down from the bridge of the *Chokai* for a cup of tea. He would drink it in the privacy of his sea cabin before the gilt-framed picture of Hirohito.

CHAPTER 6

AT 8 P.M. Admiral Mikawa's force of cruisers detected an uninvited stranger lying on the surface. Sharp-eyed lookouts bawled: "Object off the port beam! Object is enemy submarine!"

The sea was calm and the light poor. Admiral Mikawa had just come up to the *Chokai's* chart room and was discussing the forthcoming operation with Captain Mikio Hayakawa, the commanding officer of the flagship.

The alarm instantly sent the two men sprinting for the port wing, in time to see the United States Navy's submarines *S-38* dipping under. Her conning tower was all that was still visible. Captain Hayakawa ordered an immediate course change to port, while anxious Japanese sailors combed the sea for the wake of enemy torpedoes. There was none.

For Lieutenant Commander H. G. Munson, the *S-38's* skipper, a prize had been lost—a far bigger prize than he at first realized. But Munson, a veteran submariner of Captain Cristie's Task Force 42 out of Brisbane, was no man to belabor his bad luck. He promptly did the next best thing to firing torpedoes. Ordering the radio shack to tune the transmitter, Munson quickly drafted a contact report, set it in code, and got off a message telling of "two destroyers and three larger ships of unknown type" moving southeasterly at high speed.

While greatly inaccurate because of the failing evening light, this message was actually the second such sighting of Mikawa's gunships. The first, by B-17's of MacArthur's command, was the sighting of Crudiv 6 en route to the point of rendezvous.

Mikawa was too busy with details to waste time worrying. His eight ships, intact and steaming at 30 knots, had a date with destiny which was not to be put off, despite alarms and ill omens. He returned to the chart room and his discussion with Captain Hayakawa. A few members of the staff joined the two men.

Broadly speaking, Mikawa's ships could bring an awesome amount of firepower to bear: 34 8-inch (20-cm) guns; 10 5.5-inch (14-cm) guns; 27 5-inch and 4.7-inch guns; and 62 torpedo tubes. And all ships were equipped with powerful searchlights fore and aft. Because Japan lagged in the radar race, night-fighting tactics had been developed by the fleet to a fine point.

Her seamen could pinpoint an object at four miles, even on a bad night; her night binoculars were far superior to anything that the enemy possessed, and her parachute flares always worked well under any circumstances. But of foremost value was her torpedo, the dreaded Long Lance, which had a 24-inch diameter and could carry 1,000 pounds of explosive 11 miles at 49 knots,or 20 miles at 36 knots. This beat anything that the enemy could fire. The American torpedo, by comparison, could only accomodate a 750-pound charge 3 miles at 45 knots, or 7.5 miles at 26.5 knots. Further, the enemy torpedoes at this juncture of the war were thoroughly undependable, while the Japanese were perfect.

Curiously, it was a Japanese scientist, Dr. Hidetsugu Yagi, who had developed the directional antenna, as far back as 1932, but nothing was ever done about this remarkable gear by the Imperial Navy until too late. Both the United States and Great Britain had availed themselves of Yagi's invention, installing "bedsprings" aboard fighting ships at the outset of the war. However, it was only two days before the Battle of Midway that radar installations were made aboard the battleships *Ise* and *Hyuga*. This was not nearly enough.

Had Admiral Nagumo's Midway force been equipped with radar, it would not have been hampered by a dense fog and might have approached the battle area earlier. Radar might have turned the tide at Midway; but the two installations were covering such widely divergent areas that it really didn't matter.

Admiral Mikawa spent the better part of the evening in the chart room, retiring at eleven and leaving orders to be awakened at 5:15, in time for launching of the morning reconnaissance flight. He had worked out a tentative battle plan, but delayed relaying it to the other ships pending the reports of his pilots. Meanwhile, the cruiser force continued to make knots; the sea was glassy smooth, and a light breeze was wafting down from the north.

"The men are confident and, under the circumstances, secure," Captain Toshikazae Ohmae reported before the admiral left the bridge.

The night passed uneventfully.

At 5:15 an orderly tapped on the admiral's door. Mikawa was on his feet instantly to admit the caller. A pot of tea and a bowl of rice were deposited on his desk, while he hurriedly splashed water on his face and slipped on a shirt. After the makeshift breakfast Mikawa quickly went to the flag bridge to join his staff as the float planes prepared to leave the catapults.

The morning was clear and warm. On the flag bridge, Mikawa looked out over the force of warships and suddenly had visions of a flight of enemy bombers appearing from the south. The thought prompted him to tell Captain Hayakawa to, "Order Crudiv 6 to drop back a few miles and spread out at intervals of fifteen degrees." Mikawa was obviously still harboring throughts of Midway as he watched the last of four heavy cruisers disappear over the horizon.

At six o'clock the *Chokai* launched her float plane from Catapult No. 1. The charge sent the little silver-tipped plane dipping low over the water for a moment, then rising steadily and veering on course to south'ard. Sounds of the other launchings wafted across the glassy Pacific from the horizon. Mikawa and his staff remained on the bridge to enjoy a brief moment of relaxation. It was shirt-sleeve weather and the sun, just climbing out of the sea, cast its warmth over the gray steel decks where working parties labored to prepare the flagship for battle.

"I would give anything," remarked Commander Shigeru Hara enthusiastically, "to have a couple of bombs and be aboard one of those planes!"

Mikawa feigned anger. "Outbreaks of disloyalty to the Eighth Fleet will not be overlooked, Hara!" he said in a loud voice.

But there were things yet to be done, and the staff adjourned to breakfast before the day's work commenced in CIC.

To the left of *Chokai* was the *Tenryu*, and to the right the *Yubari*, light cruisers; riding ahead at a distance of two miles, with her sound gear trained out (though not much but water noise could be heard at these speeds, was the ancient warrior, the destroyer *Yunagi*. They were strange-looking ships: *Chokai*, 600 feet long and displacing 10,000 tons with her triple hull, had a fat stack that curled rakishly back and

nearly touched a thin stand-up stack. Pagoda masts gave the
ship a topheavy appearance. The light cruisers were long and
thin, two stack-jobs with upturned risers and sharply-flared
bows, bristling with anti-aircraft guns. The *Yunagi* was sharply
flared forward, her thin stacks almost meeting over a 12-cm
gun. Nevertheless, she was capable of 34 knots on four mains.
The appearance of the four cruisers was equally bizarre—and
deadly. Before another sun would rise over the Solomons, the
striking power of these quaint-looking ships would be painfully clear.

Admiral Mikawa and his staff worked out details of the
attack all morning. Occasionally the admiral wandered into
main radio to ask the chief petty officer if there had been
any word from the planes. There was none.

Mikawa didn't enjoy silence at a moment like this, and he
roamed the bridge of the *Chokai* for some moments "walking
off his anger." His continence was rewarded about 15 minutes
later when Captain Ohmae rushed up with the first of several
messages from the Aoba's pilot. At ten o'clock, he reported
that "an enemy battleship, four cruisers and seven destroyers"
were sighted to the north of Guadalcanal. Thirty minutes later
he reported that "there are fifteen transports to the north." The
pilot evidently flew over Tulagi, for there was a third report of
"two enemy heavy cruisers, twelve destroyers and three transports."

Now the staff went to work analyzing the messages. For
certain, the reports spelled the failure of the morning air
strikes from Rabaul to sink any of the enemy ships; they also
meant that no enemy carriers were anywhere within a hundred miles of Guadalcanal. But Mikawa wasn't content to rely
on the information contained in the one pilot's report, and soon
he broke radio silence and called the 25th Air Flotilla to learn
what he could from them. Although his message was received,
Mikawa got no reply until much later.

Meanwhile, there were new developments to try the admiral's patience. At 10:26 an Australian Hudson bomber
broke out of the halcyon skies above the task force, shadowing
a few minutes while Mikawa's force frantically commenced
making 90-degree turns to the northwest. The Hudson finally
disappeared and, fifteen minutes later, the cruisers recovered
their aircraft. Now another worry appeared: a low-flying
Hudson came in from the south, moving directly toward the
Japanese force. It took main battery fire from all the guns to

drive this intruder off. By now the admiral was frankly worried.

Was there anything to be gained in pressing the attack, inasmuch as the presence of the task force had been revealed? Did the sightings mean that carrier aircraft would roar in over the horizon from the Solomons? Was there any advantage in a daytime arrival? When was the best time, in view of the new developments? Would the enemy be ready?

There were no faint hearts on the *Chokai*. The swords of the samurai were unsheathed.

The meeting in the chart room was adjourned and all ships plodded onward at 24 knots, figuring on arrival at Guadalcanal about midnight or shortly thereafter. The sea was dead calm and visibility was still good.

Admiral Mikawa signaled his battle plan at 4:30 from the yard of the flagship: "We will penetrate south of Savo Sound and torpedo the enemy main force at Guadalcanal. Thence we will move toward the forward area at Tulagi and strike with torpedoes and gunfire, after which we will withdraw to the north of Savo Island."

It was a bold, ambitious plan which, for success, required the element of consistent luck. And Mikawa was still holding the hand with the four aces. Even now, an hour later, this luck was evident. A mast appeared on the horizon. It could have been *any* ship, an enemy carrier perhaps, but lookouts perceived at 30,000 meters that the silhouette was that of the aircraft tender *Akitsushima,* of the Eleventh Fleet, en route to establish a seaplane base at Gizo, in Vella Gulf.

In the *Chokai's* radio shack, flag communications officers were listening to "loud and clear" enemy plain-language transmissions from the unlocated American carriers. These were the conversations of pilots approaching the landing pattern. They told of "Green base and Red base" flight decks with the casual certainty for which they were famed. Such talk disturbed Admiral Mikawa, as it must have others on his staff. It meant that these carriers were somewhere close, even if they hadn't been discovered by Japanese pilots.

At 6:30 every ship in the Imperial force was ordered to "jettison all deckside flammables in preparation for battle." This was an order the enemy ships could well afford to copy, although they did not. It was getting dark now, and Captain Ohmae drafted a message for the admiral. Immediately a signal was blinkered to every ship in the force:

"In the finest tradition of the Imperial Navy, we shall

engage the enemy in night battle. Every man is expected to do his best."

Radio interceptions stopped about this time, but the hopes of the onrushing ships did not. Like prowling cats, darkness gave them a sense of security. Morale soared when the shack reported a message from Rabaul telling of a good strike against the enemy. Planes were supposed to have sunk two heavy and two light cruisers, and a transport.

As the fading light merged into darkness, the ships fell into battle formation—a single column of death riding at 1,200-meter intervals. A day which might have seen the destruction of the Japanese attack force had ended fortuitously. The next few hours were spent by Mikawa's men in serious thought or in writing letters to loved ones—feeling the prebattle sentimentality which affects nearly all fighting men. The admiral himself went below to his sea cabin to sip a cup of tea, and to ask the Emperor again for victory.

At 11:10 the five planes were again catapulted aloft. Admiral Mikawa wanted the enemy ships illuminated, and illuminated they soon would be. But it was strange and risky business, sending off planes from a catapult launching in the darkness, and the men held their breaths till the launching was completed. Meanwhile, Mikawa had returned to the bridge and was standing alone on a wingtip, staring ahead. In the crow's nests of the eight ships were the finest lookouts of the Eighth Fleet. The night was warm and black; the sea was brisking up. Wind was out of the southwest at four knots. The admiral went to the *Chokai's* chart room.

At 11:30 the first of the sporadic squalls which Mikawa's forces would encounter tonight struck. The wind heightened to 30 knots and then dropped off again, but occasional gusts riffled the long white streamers flying from the yard of each ship for identification purposes, and made them stand out stiff and ghostly. Speed now was upped to 26 knots. In the radio shack, the voices of the three pilots suddenly wheezed over the loudspeaker:

"Three enemy cruisers patrolling off the eastern entrance of Savo Sound!"

Mikawa promptly sent his crew rushing to battle stations. It was midnight. Speed was upped to 28 knots. An electric tension coursed through the compartments of his ship, of every ship, as all hands realized that battle was only minutes away. On the bridge the telephone talkers reported all compartments in readiness, all guns manned. Their voices were muffled but could still be heard above the variety of sounds floating in from the radio shack abaft the bridge. Mikawa came out from the chart house and stood a moment near the helmsman. But he could see little, so he decided to return to the starboard wing until the battle opened.

At 12:40 Savo Island appeared, 20 degrees on the port bow. "Ship approaching thirty degrees starboard!" a lookout growled through a voice tube.

On the flagbridge, all breathing seemed to stop. An enemy destroyer was crossing *Chokai*'s bow at 10,000 meters! Japanese gunners trained in on the American as an order flashed down from the bridge to stand by for action. Mikawa raced to the chart house in time to join a discussion of whether they should attack the target, or whether they were, sailing into an ambush.

"Left full rudder. Slow to twenty-two knots!" Mikawa personally settled the discussion. He amended the order to left rudder ten degrees. Oblivious to the steel that might have been rained down upon her then, had Mikawa willed it, the American destroyer ambled slowly on her way. The aces held in Mikawa's thin sinewy hands were apparent to every man in the Japanese task force. With no warning from the lookouts, the men on *Chokai*'s bridge watched incredulously as the destroyer reversed her course. Fantastic!

Now there was a lookout report to the bridge: "Ship sighted, twenty degrees port."

The binoculars in Mikawa's hands shifted instantly. Sure enough—a second destroyer was plodding along on patrol, moving away from the Japanese force!

"Right rudder. Steer course a hundred-fifty degrees!" Mikawa snapped. And suddenly all hands realized how close they had come to being discovered. How unbelievably close!

Dead ahead, reflected by the low-hanging clouds, leaped the flames from a burning American ship. The day's strike, thought Mikawa jubilantly, had hit something after all. But this presented a new problem to the wizards of the chart room. If the enemy were reflected in the glow of flames, then they too were.

Mikawa was resolute. He would press the attack, regardless of hazards.

At 1:30 he spat out his attack order. His force was now south of Savo Island. There the three enemy cruisers which his planes had reported were waiting to be destroyed.

Admiral Mikawa pushed up speed to 30 knots, at the same

time ordering the destroyer *Yunagi* to fall back to the rear and attack the destroyers just avoided. Captain Ohmae moved to Mikawa's side. He had plotted the location of the ships as reported by the pilots of the three planes. The admiral squinted tensely at the chart. Above the two men, a voice suddenly shattered the silence of the bridge:

"Cruiser, seven degrees port!"

Wheeling, the admiral brought up his glasses. The target was not a cruiser but a destroyer. And then came the report Mikawa had been yearning to hear:

"Three cruisers, nine degrees starboard, moving to the right!"

A parachute flare abruptly illuminated the target in stark brilliance. Range, 8,000 meters!

Admiral Mikawa's order was crisp: "Torpedoes fire to starboard. *Fire!*"

Almost immediately, the dull *thwack* of torpedoes striking the water was heard. With rapier swiftness Mikawa moved to the open bridge, fixing his night glasses on the targets. In the radio shack a communicator thumbed the intercom and reported that all ships had fired with guns and torpedoes. At this moment Admiral Mikawa saw the flash of a salvo and heard the roar of a torpedo striking a target broad on the beam. It was 1:37 A.M.

CHAPTER 7

OPERATION WATCHTOWER had weathered two rugged days in the Solomons. Admiral Turner's outfit, Task Force 62, had commenced unloading Marines and the materials of war at H-hour, 9:10 A.M. of D-day, after a naval bombardment which leveled most of the enemy installations on Tulagi and Guadalcanal. There was no opposition on Guadalcanal. The enemy had lit out for the hills.

The first casualty of the campaign was a Marine. He was killed when a rifle accidentally discharged aboard the destroyer-transport *Little*. A burial detail took the body ashore later in the morning. Someone said it was a shame that he couldn't have gotten it on the beach, the right way.

Turner's force was split into two groups: X-ray and Yoke. The Guadalcanal transports (X-ray) were the *Fuller, American Legion, Bellatrix, McCawley* (the flagship), *Barnett, Elliot, Libra, Hunter, Ligett, Alchida, Fomalhaut, Betelgeuse, Crescent City, President Hayes, President Adams* and *Alhena*. The Tulagi transports (Yoke) were the *Neville, President Jackson, Calhoun, Zeilin, Haywood, Gregory, Little* and *McKean*. The last four-named vessels were destroyer escorts.

A few minutes before the first wave of Marines stepped ashore at Guadalcanal, the *Astoria*'s plane flew over the beachhead. The pilot first reported "no activity," but quickly amended the report to read "several Jap trucks moping along Lunga Field." This was news enough for General Vandergrift, aboard the flagship with Turner. He put in a hurry call to the *Saratoga*. There were Japs a few thousand yards from where his troops were landing, and he wanted them out of the way.

It was done. A flight of VS-3's roared over the spot ten minutes later and the hazard was neutralized. The carrier fly-boys were always happy to oblige.

In that first wave ashore was the correspondent Richard Tregaskis, who hardly got his shoes wet jumping off the boat.

An Australian Army captain confided as they sat under a coconut tree, "I'm exhausted by the arduousness of landing against such heavy fire." He would swallow his sarcasm when the Marines reached the Tenaru River.

The prelanding objective of the first wave was "Grassy Knoll," a misnomer about 1,500 feet high, sometimes referred to in Marine histories as Mount Asten. A rugged, truncated mass, it lay about ten miles from the Lunga beachhead, and was separated from it by rivers, jungles, kunai plains, gorges and steep ravines, all overgrown with virtually impenetrable verdure.

Colonel Cates, the Marine CO, promptly advised General Vandergrift of the situation. The general sent back:

"Hike no more. Select new objective."

The beach finally chosen lay about 9,000 yards southeast of Lunga Point, not far from the original landing. Float planes from the *Astoria* and *Quincy* marked the extremities of the beachhead; at the same time they served as spotters. But there wasn't anything to spot.

By noon a command post for Admiral Turner was being prepared by Marines, and heavy equipment was coming ashore. The enemy had still not been met, although Intelligence estimated (overestimated) that there were 5,000 troops on the island. Most of these were construction battalions, men who had been employed in the building of airstrips.

But on Tulagi and the harbor islands of Gavutu and Tanambogo, where H-hour was set ahead 70 minutes, the situation was anything but peaceful. A lusty scrap, begun that morning, was still in progress. Here was the 3rd Kure Special Landing Force, the enemy's elite amphibious troops. These few rifles put up a whopping good fight, despite a strike by fifteen *Wasp* aircraft and a pinpoint bombardment by the destroyers *Monssen* and *Buchanan* and the light cruiser *San Juan*.

"Enemy force is overwhelming. We will defend our positions to the death," the Tulagi garrison had radioed to Rabaul.

Now they intended to prove it.

Major Lloyd Nickerson's first wave (Company B) hit the beach to the accompaniment of a retreating but nevertheless rattling hail of machine-gun fire. In this wave was Major Justice Chambers (Company D) and his leatherneck veterans. These men were Raiders, specially assigned by Marine planning to the toughest fighting areas. Behind them was the second wave (Companies A and C), also chafing for a fight.

As the Marines scrambled ashore, the enemy retreated into the woody, hilly, cave-pocked terrain. The Marines went in after them. Fighting lasted all day and throughout the night. Many of the Japs were hidden in large caves which connected with other caves by a series of tunnels. As quickly as the Marines would blast them out of one, they reappeared in another. It was a slow, tortuous process, and each Jap fought until he was killed.

"They were lousy shots," Chambers said later. "If they had been good shots, a damn sight more of us would have died."

Outside the harbor where she was plastering Hill 208, cruiser *San Juan* got a sound contact on one of the submarines Admiral Mikawa had diverted from a routine sea lane patrol. She promptly broke off bombardment and attacked with depth charges. After two run-ins, an oil slick appeared and *San Juan* turned tail, leaving the balance of the job to destroyers. Hill 201 was her most important neutralization mission, and that hill—even with naval gunfire—had to be taken by rifles and grenades, the hard way. It was the same rugged story on Halavao, a miniscule island in the harbor.

At Gavutu the 1st Parachute Battalion, also doing it the hard way, came in by boats from the *Heywood,* a seven-mile run through choppy seas from the line of departure. The Higgins Boat Company designed a hull for rough water, but it didn't design the stomachs of men. Many in the 1st Parachute Battalion were seasick and doubtless wished that the landings could have been accomplished from the air.

Enfilading fire coming from the beach where Japs were hidden in coconut-tree bunkers, and from a partially sunken flying boat, caught the first wave along the south side of the island and nearly wiped out the entire contingent. Kure Marines would let the Americans reach the beachhead, then catch them in murderous crossfire as they raced across the open sands. Time and again this happened. Marines coming in from the line of departure were caught on the coral heads in the Higgins boats. As the boats frantically attempted to back off, the Japanese swiveled their fire from the beach to the water.

Brigadier General William H. Rupertus, the tough, taciturn second-in-command under Vandergrift, was in charge of the assault troops at Tulagi and the harbor islands. Rupertus was no armchair general. He made the beachhead assault with wet feet and a blazing automatic, which was par for the course in that area. The small green islands across from quiet Guadalcanal, where 11,000 troops would disembark before nightfall, gave the special assault troops their toughest assignment.

The fourth wave was going ashore at Beach Red, between Lunga and Koli points, which Colonel Cates had decided was the logical place for a landing and mass staging area. Now the Marines were in the jungle, following the enemy Japs.

"We would bump into something very shortly after we got ashore," was the way Major Donald Dickson put it to correspondent Karig. "The men had moved inward, but there was still no answering fire from the enemy. We crossed a field of grass which was about shoulder high, moved inland for probably one and a half to two miles. We had to cross the Ilu River, and that was one of those things we had looked forward to with a little worry, because we understood the Ilu River had rather steep banks and a very muddy bottom, and we didn't quite know how we were going to bridge it. But one of our brilliant boys, I don't know who it was, suggested we build bridges on top of the amphtracks; I think that was an example of somebody using his head. Still no enemy fire, but it would come soon enough."

Afloat, Admiral Ghormley's forces were patrolling the beachheads and delivering up a blistering fire whenever required. At Bougainville, the head end of the Solomons, a coastwatcher saw Japanese bombers taking off on the first retaliatory strike from Rear Admiral Yamada's 25th Air Flotilla at Rabaul. He unzipped his portable teleradio and flashed: "From STO. Twenty-four torpedo bombers headed yours." The warning was received by the transports and their screening ships in plenty of time.

Aboard the HMAS *Canberra*, moving down Sealark Channel after the earlier bombardment, the sweet shrill of a bos'n's pipe over the loudspeaker system announced that there was something of importance to be heard. A moment later the voice of Captain Frank Getting boomed, "This ship will be attacked at noon by twenty-four torpedo bombers. Hands will pipe to dinner at eleven o'clock."

On this grimly humorous note, warships and transports got under way in sufficient time to stave off disaster. Admiral Turner, who had worked out a plan for evasive tactics, had his transports present the tightest possible angle of fire to the Japanese gunners by lying parallel to the beaches. He now ordered them to get under way. The enemy sortie was picked up by the *Chicago's* radar at 43 miles; the Japanese bombs all fell wide of targets. A few minutes after the raid was over the transports returned to unload.

On Guadalcanal, Admiral Turner's beach headquarters was ready and the admiral obligingly climbed into his barge and came ashore. Shooting was yet to begin on this island, but at Tulagi, Gavutu and Tanambogo, where it had been raging since midday, 108 Marines were killed and 140 wounded. Except for snipers, who resisted all efforts to be blasted out of the caves and bunkers, some 1,500 Japanese were wiped out.

At about 3 P.M., two Japanese groups which had not been picked up on radar roared in from the north. Again the result was more noise than damage. The planes scored one hit on the destroyer *Mugford* and killed 22 men but, as with the previous strike, aircraft from the *Enterprise, Wasp* and *Saratoga* met the enemy bombers in headlong attack and quickly blasted them out of the skies. Out of a group of eleven planes sent down by Admiral Yamada of the 25th Air Flotilla, all but one was shot down in flames by the F4F's. . . .

Night came to the Solomon Islands.

At Guadalcanal the enemy still refused to show himself, and Major Dickson's Marines had to spend the night lying awake in foxholes and "sweating out every strange sound. It was dangerous to get up and go to the head . . . the sentries would fire at almost anything."

On Tulagi, the 3rd Kure Special Landing Force waited for cover of darkness before shouting taunts at the Marines companies hunkered down in their foxholes. The voices were close and shrill:

"President Roosevelt die! American Marine, you die with knife! Babe Ruth is coward!"

Before an attack the Japs would always work themselves up, and then the screams would abruptly stop. There would be only the silence of the jungle, the weird cry of birds and the chattering of monkeys. Then would come the charge. Three times that first night the Japanese Marines swarmed out of the jungle screaming *"Banzai!"* and closed with bayonets. On their last charge they came within 20 yards of the perimeter.

But at Guadalcanal the Marines had to nurture their private fears a while longer. There, the worst that had happened during the day was that somebody cut his hand opening a coconut.

Here, other than a great deal of confusion on Beach Red, where Marines had stoutheartedly resisted all attempts of Captain L. F. Reifsnider, Commander of Transport Division C, to convert them into stevedores, everybody was satisfied. The beach was glutted with heavy equipment and supplies; boxes of ammunition and crates of food were piled a dozen feet high. Just about the only one who was disturbed (other than the Marine Corps) by all this was Reifsnider, who had a few choice words for the commanders of the Pioneer Battalion, which had stubbornly resisted being responsible for any thing other than hunting down the enemy. Reifsnider reported to Admiral Turner:

"A serious situation developed during the landings when the labor section of the shore party was unable to cope with the rapidity and quantity of supplies and equipment delivered at the beach. The situation is ascribed to the total lack of conception of the number of labor troops required to unload boats and move material off the beaches, failure to extend the beach limits earlier in the operation and, to some extent, lack of control of troops on and in the immediate vicinity of the beach—it was definitely understood and agreed that the unloading of the boats and the removal of the material from the beach would be done by the labor section. . . ."

In a sense Reifsnider's anger was justified. Admiral Turner's flagship alone had unloaded 100,000 cubic feet of cargo in the first nine hours, and there were 20 transports at Guadalcanal and Tulagi *exclusive* of the four-destroyer transports!

The first day was a rough one for Turner, especially. He was worried about the safety of his transports. The two air attacks, and he knew there would soon be more, had prompted him to urge Admiral McCain to send a Catalina up The Slot from Commander Ned Hitchcock's tender *Mackinac* at Malaita. This was done, but the PBY missed the sighting of the Japanes force, one reason being that the warships of Admiral Mikawa were still shaping a course to the north of Bougainville, and were not as yet actually in the head islands of the Solomons.

The warning from *S-38*, which had sighted Admiral Mikawa's force off Cape St. George, had been received. Let 'em come and catch hell! was the way some put it. There was absolutely nothing to worry about.

Nightfall brought a welcome surcease from bombardment and air raid to the warships patrolling off the beaches. Ex-

hausted sailors slept at their guns. General quarters was secured. Condition II, which allowed half the crew to sleep,
was set. There was, after all, nothing to worry about. The
invasion was safe.

CHAPTER 8

ABOARD THE warships General Quarters sounded at 4 A.M., and for the second straight day tired gunners loaded their weapons and settled down to await the coming of Japanese bombers. It was a fine dawn, clear and with just a hint of a breeze blowing out of the north. Vice Admiral Ghormley had flown up to Noumea the previous evening, but on the forenoon watch of August 8 he passed a message to all hands in the Guadalcanal area:

"Results so far achieved make every officer and man in the South Pacific proud of the task forces," said Ghormley.

However, a few of the commanders were not only proud but worried. There were rumors about that the Tokyo Express was on the way, and if this actually were the case they needed to know more.

Beetle-browed, outspoken Rear Admiral Richmond Kelly Turner, the blacksmith's son, was one who needed to know. His responsibility was the safety of the transport divisions. Rear Admiral Victor Alexander Charles Crutchley, the fiercely-bearded Englishman in command of the screening forces, was another. Crutchley, who had headed up Britain's blockading forces at Ostend during World War I, had heard the *S-38* report while at breakfast aboard his flagship, the HMAS *Australia*. Turner had passed it to him. Shortly after the submarine report Turner relayed another contact message, passed by General MacArthur's B-17's, which had spotted the Japanese task force near Bougainville. But pending the receipt of amplifying information by a closer source, neither Turner nor Crutchley could take countermeasures.

Ashore, Marines were putting the finishing touches to the scrap at Tulagi and the harbor islands. Rear Admiral Norman Scott, who carried his flag in the cruiser *San Juan*, was again called upon to deliver pinpoint fire and to pummel the Japs entrenched in the hill caves of Tulagi. At Guadalcanal, Marines were moving up to the rugged Tenaru River country and getting ready for a first-rate battle.

They had long since passed the airfield which was later called Henderson Field. "It was apparently deserted," Major Dickson told Karig. "It looked only like a large meadow. We saw one building on it which was later called the Pagoda, and we sent patrols across to that. Then we came to the first Japanese camp. I went through it with several other people, to look it over. There had been no Marines through it at all up to that time, and I could see then how the Japs had rushed off when our shelling commenced.

"They had just taken off, leaving food on the tables. There was all kinds of gear left there; blacksmiths shops, quartermaster's storerooms and garages with hundreds of bicycles—most of them with flat tires, though! There we found the Jap headquarters, and several cans of hardtack that had been opened and apparently just a few fistfuls taken out before they took off. There was also a quantity of beer and saki, a lot of Jap cigarettes and candy."

At 10:28 A.M., while Turner and Crutchley were trying to track down any information about the rumored coming of the Tokyo Express, the Australian reconnaissance flight from Milne Bay sighted Admiral Mikawa's force steaming southward. Instead of breaking radio-silence, as he was supposed to have done, the pilot of the Hudson bomber "spent most of the afternoon completing his search mission, came down at sundown," hit the tea bottle, and then, probably as an afterthought, reported the Japanese contact to MacArthur's headquarters at Brisbane!

Meanwhile, Admiral Yamada's 25th Air Flotilla was sending down another flight of torpedo bombers with orders to come in low, regardless of the cost. But this time fighter planes from the *Enterprise* were waiting. Tipped off, the ships got underway and commenced radical maneuvering. Aboard *McCawley*, Turner's flagship, which had unloaded 100,000 cubic feet of cargo in nine hours, a fighting-mad gun crew blazed away at this incoming flight with devastating results. A colored mess attendant, hunched over the sweaty handles of a 20-millimeter gun, accounted for four of the enemy bombers.

Flaming Jap twin-engine Mitsubichis crashed between the milling transports, and as the latter maneuvered in the confines of the narrow channel, lifebelts were thrown to the enemy aviators. Few took them. There was a hit aboard the *Jarvis*, a screening destroyer, but it was not fatal although it necessitated a major repair job. The big hit was aboard the transport *George F. Elliot*, the former *City of San Francisco*, where the pilot had tried *kamikaze* tactics and had managed to steer his plane into the fantail of the ship.

The *Elliot* was abandoned prematurely. Fires quickly raged out of control. Later, a destroyer was detached from the screen to put four "pickles" into the hull, but the torpedoes, fired at close range, had no effect. Destined to become a derelict, a flaming beacon, the *Elliot's* fires would shortly guide Admiral Mikawa's cruiser force to its destination.

The enemy admitted the loss of seventeen bombers.

No air raids disrupted the unloading operations of the afternoon. About this time the pilot of the second Hudson sighted the enemy force, but again for some reason no report was made! Unhappily, in the earlier case the report was late and inaccurate, and in the later one the pilots, incredibly, just didn't bother to report.

By now Turner and Crutchley, the recipients of these vicious air attacks, were fit to be tied. The misleading earlier contact report had them believing that their forces were in for another battle with enemy planes, and because their own searches had failed to reveal the presence of Mikawa in The Slot, they assumed the enemy was hiding behind the mountains of Santa Isabelle. There was no thought of a surface action with strong Japanese forces.

"These failures in ship identification and communications," wrote Navy historian Samuel Eliot Morison, "are enough to explain why Admiral Mikawa managed to make his approach undetected."

Now a new and far more serious problem arose for Admiral Turner, the commander of the transports. Admiral Fletcher, during the midocean conference of July 26, had told Turner that because of a fueling problem he couldn't remain in the area more than two days. Turner was furious. He said he needed four days to unload. But the senior admiral was adamant.

Fletcher, roundly criticized by a *War College Analysis* for using the fuel excuse to cover up his fear of losing carriers (he had lost *Yorktown* and *Lexington* at Coral Sea and Midway), evidently had no shortage whatever. The *Saratoga*, for example, had plenty of the liquid black stuff aboard. In fact her gauges showed that there were 1,149,000 gallons aboard, despite the fact that her destroyer group was *already* topped off.

At 6:07 P.M., as the sun dipped behind Cape Esperance and only the tracers from landing Marines showed over the harbor islands, Fletcher recovered all his planes, drafted a terse explanation to Ghormley, and pulled out: "Fighter plane strength reduced from 99 to 78. In view of the large number of enemy torpedo planes and bombers in this area, I recommend the immediate withdrawal of my carriers. Request that tankers be sent forward immediately, as fuel running low. . . ."

Turner did a slow burn.

Ghormley, about a thousand miles from the scene, was in no position to dispute Fletcher's word. The commander of the amphibious forces, on the other hand, believed he was shortly to be the recipient of a Japanese air attack (the phrasing of the early contact reports indicated an enemy air sortie, rather than a surface engagement), and when he intercepted Fletcher's departing message he was further fit to be tied.

Even had Fletcher's carriers remained, as Turner hoped they would, it is rather doubtful that the outcome of the battle might have been changed. With the absence of Fletcher's aircraft carriers, a thoroughly chagrined commander of the amphibious forces crossed his fingers and issued orders to his screening force to assume night dispositions. He also alerted the commanding officers concerned to expect a Japanese air attack, or anyway an attack of some sort, before long.

Admiral Crutchley's job was to protect the transports at Guadalcanal and Tulagi, and protect them he would, even if he had to split his forces to do so. (That this was a mistake would soon become evident.) Savo Sound was divided into three sections, a Northern, Southern, and Eastern force to patrol each. The Southern Force consisted of *Australia* (Captain Harold B. Farncomb, RAN), *Canberra* (Captain Frank E. Getting, RAN), and *Chicago* (Captain Howard D. Bode), with a screen made up of destroyers *Patterson* (Commander Frank R. Walker) and *Bagley* (Lieutenant Commander George A. Sinclair).

These ships had operated together for some time, had been together at Coral Sea, and before that had made up the battle line of the old Anzac force. They were familiar with all the maneuvers and tactics that are required for units to operate together as a main body. Their patrol was a line "running 125 degrees from the center of Savo Island, to block the entrance between it and Cape Esperance."

The Northern Force, patrolling north of the line "to block the entrance between Savo and Florida Islands," consisted of cruisers *Vincennes* (Captain Frederick L. Riefkohl), *Astoria* (Captain William G. Greenman) and *Quincy* (Captain Samuel N. Moore), with destroyers *Helm* (Lieutenant Commander Chester E. Carroll) and *Wilson* (Lieutenant Commander Walter H. Price) screening. This force was under the tactical command of Captain Reifkohl—"Fearless Freddy" to the men of the *Vincennes*. Radar pickets *Blue* (Commander Harold N. Williams) and *Ralph Talbot,* destroyers, were to cover both approaches to the sound.

The Eastern Force, commanded by Rear Admiral Norman Scott in the *San Juan,* was composed of HMAS *Hobart* (Captain Henry A. Showers, RAN), another light cruiser, with screening destroyers *Monssen* (Captain Roland N. Smoot), and *Buchanan* (Commander Ralph E. Wilson).

With Fletcher retiring, and the Japs advancing, it was Admiral Turner's intention to unload the transports all night.

Unfortunately, this would not be done under cover of darkness. The *Elliot,* still flaming, was a bright light to the stevedores . . . and to Admiral Mikawa. At this moment Turner, who was already upset, received the famous Hudson sighting report and blew his stack. The message had come by way of "Bells" the Australian equivalent of the "Fox Sked," a routine Navy broadcast from Brisbane: "Three cruisers, three destroyers, two seaplane tenders or gunboats, course 120 degrees, speed fifteen knots."

Eight hours for a mesage to come a few hundred miles!

Admiral Turner did what he could under the circumstances. While the ships were patrolling the entrance to Savo Sound— without a battle plan, for there had been no time in which Admiral Crutchley could have drawn one—a conference was quickly called aboard the transport—flagship *McCawley.* To this conference came Crutchley, who pulled *Australia* out of the Southern Force line, and Vandergrift.

Turner, the distressed commander of the amphibious forces, wanted to discuss Admiral Fletcher's southward withdrawal with these points in mind: 1) Could the Marines unload all the transports this night, or did they prefer to take a beating from Japanese bombers? 2) Could the fighting ships stick it out without air cover for two more days, if necessary?

It was 10:30 P. M. Captain Howard D. Bode swung the

Chicago to the head of the line abandoned by the *Australia*. The calm, clear weather had changed (an augury?) and now the ships were riding in "hot, oppressive weather," pregnant with squalls.

Crutchley arrived aboard *McCawley* first from his barge, and 45 minutes later the Marine general appeared. The three men were exhausted from the strain of the two days, and they showed it. It was Vandergrift's impression about now that he was "pretty tired, but as for those other two, I thought they were both ready to pass out."

The commander of the amphibious forces wasted no time. It was his proposal that the transports pull out the next morning. The three men agreed. Vandergrift, however, expressed dissatisfaction that his Marines be left ashore with inadequate supplies and no naval support. Crutchley at this time asked Turner about the belated report that had come over "Bells" from the Hudson pilot. Turner said that the Japs would likely hole up at a nearby bay and launch torpedo bomber strikes from that point. He said that he had requested additional help from Admiral McCain's land-based aircraft, and that help was forthcoming; he also mentioned a possibility of a sea attack.

The conference was still in session as the men on the warships settled down to an uneasy rest. Condition II had been set. On the *Vincennes*, Chaplain (Lieutenant Commander) George Schwyhart, who had grown up in Iowa and had gone to sea first on the old battleship *Wyoming*, came down to the wardroom to join several officers at a late evening mess.

After dinner the men sat around discussing the rumors of a Jap movement to the south. The concensus was that the enemy was walking into a death trap. Or was he? The more the men talked about it, the less confident they became. Finally, talk stopped entirely, and Schwyhart and the ship's doctor, Commander James D. Blackwood, sixty, went for a breath of air.

Here the men could see Marine tracers spraying the harbor islands, and fires burning on the beach. Blackwood talked about his department:

"If something should ever happen, the medical department has been tested and found not wanting."

It was 11:30. A squall was making up off Savo Island, and a wet Stygian curtain began to blot out vision between the patrolling groups. Some men slept topside at their guns, others on deck curled up in sheltered places. Aboard the *McCawley* the conference was breaking up.

On the radar picket *Ralph Talbot,* to the westward of Savo

Island, a lookout suddenly shouted to the bridge that there was a plane moving over the sound. This aircraft was identified as the float type carried aboard Japanese cruisers. Then, over the destroyer's TBS, came the tocsin: "Warning—warning: Plane over Savo, headed east."

CHAPTER 9

CAPTAIN FRANK GETTING, a conscientious and capable officer, prowled the darkened bridge of HMAS *Canberra*. With him were Lieutenant Commander Plunkett-Cole, torpedo officer, Lieutenant Commander Hole, gunnery officer, and Lieutenant Commander Mesley, navigator. The Australian heavy cruiser was steaming at the head of the Southern Force.

A fresh duty section relieved the watch at 11:45 and was again reminded of the possibility of an enemy attack. Despite a few hours of sleep, these men were still tense and exhausted after two days of seemingly incessant air raids and bombardment. Astern was the heavy cruiser *Chicago,* distant 600 yards, Captain Howard Bode commanding.

Shortly before, when Admiral Crutchley had pulled HMAS *Australia* out of the line in order to attend Admiral Turner's conference, Bode automatically became OTC (Officer in Tactical Command) and should have moved to the head of the column. But Getting, like Bode—who thought it really didn't matter, since Crutchley would be returning soon anyway—had no particular objection to the present arrangements.

"Nothing to report," noted *Canberra's* log at the beginning of the midwatch.

An affable, moon-faced man, Frank Getting had been to sea since boyhood. In another year or so he was scheduled to go up to flag rank. The 9,850-ton *Canberra,* commissioned in 1928 as one of the first Australian ships built under the Naval Armament Treaty agreement, was his first gunship command. Getting liked the way the high-sided, three-stack cruiser handled herself. She was old, true enough, but among the Anzac forces she had earned the repuation of being a trim, taut ship, and the captain aimed to keep her reputation spotless.

Only forty-three, Getting was regarded as one of the Royal Australian Navy's promising CO's (commanding officers). His last ship, HMAS *Kanimbla,* an armed merchant cruiser operating out of the China Station, was a stubby converted freighter. Under Getting's fine hand, however, *Kanimbla* became a veritable battleship, while her commanding officer made for himself the reputation of being a swashbuckler.

"Ting" Getting, although his patrol was fairly quiet under normal conditions, was not a man to keep things calm for long. His gunboat soon became embroiled in two international incidents which caused a diplomatic uproar. The first was in connection with the removal of "German nationals" from the Japanese freighter *Asama Maru* (it was still a one-ocean war). The second incident, the overhauling of the Russian *V. Mayakovsky* because Getting suspected a contraband cargo, erupted into open controversy.

Not long after, Getting went on a tour at naval headquarters where, it was finally deduced, he had the makings of a fine admiral. After all, he had only done his duty—perhaps a bit too energetically to please everybody, but he had done it nevertheless. Three years later, Getting was assigned to the heavy cruiser *Canberra,* which was operating on the convoy lanes in the Maldive Island-Sumamra grid.

Now, shortly after midnight as the opening round of the battle of Savo was about to commence, Getting told Lieutenant Commander Mesley, "It's quiet now. I'll slip into my cabin for a few winks." He quickly took leave of the white-clad figures pacing the bridge, and retired to his stateroom abaft the wheelhouse. Everything was normal. The last words that Getting was to hear before the clanging of the general alarm sent the crew racing to battle stations were, "Port fifteen degrees rudder"—a nice, comforting command.

"An aircraft was heard at infrequent intervals from about 2300 (eleven o'clock) onward. Type 271 RDF was in operation but interference from surrounding land minimized its efficiency," the navigator recorded a few moments after the captain departed. (This was Mikawa's float planes spotting before they dropped flares.)

In air defense high above the bridge, lookouts sensed a coming change of weather. No longer was it clear and balmy. Now the blanket of low-hanging thunderheads obscured Savo Island and Tulagi. Lieutenant Thomas Logan, in sky control, called to the bridge and asked if there were any noticeable drop in the glass. There was, the navigator reported, but it probably didn't mean anything "as the weather is always changing around here." Logan settled down to an uneasy watch. In a moment he would feel the rain.

Astern was the reassuring silhouette of the *Chicago*. Captain Howard Bode, fifty-three, had assumed command upon the loss of his last ship, the *Oklahoma,* at Pearl Harbor. That day Bode had missed death by a whisker when the battleship capsized under the impact of Japanese torpedoes and bombs. But tonight his luck would run out, and more than a year after Savo Island was written into history, he would commit suicide.

"Ironbottom Sound" would be the undoing of this career officer, who was scheduled to move up to flag rank. His death, listed in Navy biographies as "Not a war casualty," would occur at the NOB (Naval Operating Base) in Balboa, Panama. Gunichi Mikawa's sting would carry with it a virulence even after eight months and at a distance of several thousand miles!

Bode, upon Crutchley's retirement, "directed formation to remain where it was," and slipped below to his sea cabin. Like the man, the ship had also rubbed shoulders with death in this war. Commissioned in 1931, the 9,300-ton *Chicago* was the second United States Navy ship to bear this name. The Honorable Fred A. Britten, congressman from Illinois, was the sparkplug who fired the move to build this cruiser, and his sister, Miss Elizabeth Britten, was given the honor of breaking the champagne bottle across her prow.

In November of 1941 the *Chicago* was engaged with various task forces developing tactics and cruising formations out of Pearl Harbor. When the news of the Japanese attack was received, the ship was at sea with Task Force 12.

Immediately she commenced a high-speed sweep to the southeastward in the Oahu-Johnston-Palmyra triangle, in an effort to intercept the enemy. There was no enemy to be found. Three months later her luck turned. In February, *Chicago* arrived at Suva Bay and joined the newly-formed Anzac forces commanded by Vice Admiral R. F. Leary. After carrying this officer's three-star flag for only a month, however, the heavy cruiser was transferred to Task Force 2, under the command of Vice Admiral Wilson Brown. This force was to attack and destroy enemy forces at Lae and Salamau, New Guinea, by air attacks from the Gulf of Papau.

On May 4, when the Battle of Coral Sea was only hours away, *Chicago* supported the carrier planes of *Yorktown,* which inflicted heavy damage on enemy forces landing at Tulagi. Now she was blooded. Attacked by eleven single-engine land-based planes, *Chicago's* hot gunners promptly drove them off, downing three in the process. The following day another flight of twelve bombers came down from Rabaul and the *"Chi's"* blistering fire claimed five of them.

Captain Bode, her wartime commanding officer, infused in the crew a fighting spirit and determination which carried down to the lowest-ranking sailor. The men were proud of the ship, and rightfully so. She had dodged Japanese torpedoes in Sydney Harbor, had killed one midget submarine and driven off another when the enemy attempted their abortive attack on that port. She had fought with commendable enthusiasm and "rated" the fine reputation carried among the ships of the fleet. But now, as the staunch little figure of Gunichi Mikawa loomed on the horizon, *Chicago's* lucky streak would end. This time she would not dodge a torpedo.

It was 1 A.M. and the Japanese admiral's cruisers were south of Savo Island—eight deadly gunships steaming in a single line.

Destroyer *Blue,* her SC (search) radar apparently trained in every direction but the right one—astern—was headed southwesterly at a leisurely pace, oblivious of the drama in which she had suddenly become the star.

Aboard the enemy ships all guns trained on the *Blue,* ready to snuff out her life in an instant hail of steel should the tin can make an alarming movement. Mikawa's force, steaming at 26 knots, moved deeper toward the anchorage and passed to the north of Savo Island, unnoticed. Somewhere ahead, Mikawa knew, were the three fat American cruisers which had been reported by his pilots.

"Steer course 150 degrees," Mikawa ordered.

Now only a few minutes remained before he would give the command for "independent firing!" *Blue* disappeared astern.

Ahead in the darkness were the ships of the Southern Force: *Canberra* and *Chicago,* with destroyers *Bagley* and *Patterson* forming a close A/S (anti-submarine) screen. The tin cans were positioned on the port and starboard bows of the leading vessel. Mikawa didn't see these ships yet, but at 26 knots it wouldn't be long before he did.

"Seas smooth with easterly winds, skies overcast with intermittent showers, no moon. Ship darkened and in material condition affirm. All armament manned," recorded *Bagley's* quartermaster.

Commander George A. Sinclair, C.O. of the *Craven*-class destroyer, a 1,500-ton vessel built in 1937 and named for a destroyer lost in the Spanish-American War, was on the bridge. Sinclair had been aboard her since Pearl Harbor.

Among the first ships to open fire at enemy planes on December 7, at that time *Bagley* was moored at Berth 22-B for repairs to her starboard bilge keel. Her crew sped to battle stations as enemy bombers peeled off and launched a torpedo into the helpless *Oklahoma.* Sinclair fought his ship successfully until nine that morning, when the destroyer got under way, standing to seaward in a millrace of exploding battlewagons and blistering fire. Only once did *Bagley* stop, and this was to pluck from the water several men, among them the skipper of the *Patterson.*

Later, as one of the supporting ships of Vice Admiral Fletcher's *Lexington,* at Coral Sea, *Bagley*'s guns claimed several enemy planes.

Destroyer *Patterson*'s naval career paralleled that of *Bagley*. A single-stack *Craven*-class vessel named for Commodore Daniel Todd Patterson, a hero of the Battle of New Orleans in 1813, she was floated into commission at Bremerton, Washington, in a twin ceremony with her sister ship the *Jarvis.*

Patterson's anti-aircraft batteries had accounted for one "kill" at Pearl Harbor. Thereafter she participated in the raid on Rabaul, in the same action, which saw Lieutenant (jg) E. H. "Butch" O'Hare shoot down five enemy planes. Then came the raid on New Guinea with Task Force 11, and her "blooding" was complete.

These were the ships of the Southern Force which looked to Captain Howard Bode for leadership. At 11:10 the British admiral, Crutchley, aboard HMAS *Australia,* had departed. He had sent by blinker tube:

> "TAKE CHARGE OF PATROL X AM CLOSING COMTASKFOR 62 AND MAY OR MAY NOT REJOIN YOU LATER X."

Take charge? Captain Bode of the *Chicago* was no man to bother with trivialities. Why bother moving out of formation when Crutchley would return? He stalked about the bridge until the watch was relieved and then went to his cabin. Nothing was going to happen tonight. . . .

At 1:30 the Japanese commander altered course to 95 degrees. In the plotting room of the flagship, a tense knot of officers listened to their admiral's order wafting over the inter-com from the open bridge:

"All ships attack!"

It was at this precise moment that the wounded destroyer *Jarvis* was seen standing out to sea. Once again the Japanese gunners trained their batteries around, but nothing happened! *Jarvis* was silent. Her antenna had been damaged during the aerial attack in the afternoon. Even if she were able to see the Mikawa caravan, she was powerless to use her radio. Her communications system was gone, as she herself would be in a few hours when another flight of bombers would come down from Rabaul, spot an *"Achilles*-class cruiser," and proceed to sink her with all hands. . . .

Mikawa passed on. At 1:36 his lookouts saw the silhouettes of destroyers *Patterson* and *Bagley*, nearing the end of their patrol and closing at 36 knots on a collision course. Japanese torpedoes were away at this moment, spearing out for the ships of the Southern Force. It was the *Patterson* who saw the enemy van first. Over the intership-communication sys-tem (TBS) came the tocsin:

"Warning! Warning! Strange ships entering the harbor!"

But it was already too late. Even as this call was going out over the airwaves, Japanese float planes were dropping their flares. A brilliant, ghostly white series of lights floated down to illuminate the anchorage and the screening ships *Canberra* and *Chicago*.

"Independent firing!" Mikawa boomed.

At 1:37 the *Chokai* and two other cruisers opened up for-ward. High in the foremast of the Australian cruiser, Able Seaman A. B. Mackintosh saw the loom of a ship bearing down. Next he spotted the torpedo wakes, bubbly and phos-phorescent. He shouted: "Torpedoes both sides!"

Then a moment later Mackintosh saw bright flashes from the enemy cruisers' forward guns. He fairly screamed this time: "Gunfire! Dead on the starboard bow!"

Instantly the general alarm was sounded. It was still sound-ing as torpedoes slashed in on both sides of the *Canberra*. The fish to port missed; the ones to starboard didn't. The alarm started sailors racing to battle stations, while gun captains frantically trained out their batteries. It brought Captain Frank Getting to the bridge just at the moment that two fish tore into the cruiser's starboard side and the first of 24 heavy-caliber shells began to mangle the cruiser's hull.

Lieutenant Commander Hole, gunnery officer, called for

main battery fire, but before guns could be brought to bear Gunichi Mikawa's shells began falling. The high-hulled cruiser rocked as enemy fire burst along her decks and began to claw at her vitals. Fires started to spread along the entire topsides. In a turret a voice cried: "There's no electrical power to the director!" And another voice: "The dynamos have been knocked!"

The *Canberra* skidded out of formation, sent off a few rounds, and then came to a standstill in her own wake.

In the plotting room a shell exploded with a terrible roar and Captain Getting fell to the deck, mortally wounded. (He succumbed the following day.) The limp white-clad figures of the navigator and gunnery officer lay besde him, killed instantly, and nearby were five seamen who were dead or dying. The stench of cordite hung heavy in the air amid pungent black smoke and the beginning of a fire. Commander James A. Walsh, the executive officer, fought his way to the bridge from after control. He was among the rescue party which battled the incipient blaze in the chart room, from which the victims were hastily removed.

To the wheel house hurried ship's surgeon Dr. Downward. He saw the captain, propped up on a stool, and supported by Coxswain Paul Downs. Getting was drenched in his own blood, but he wasn't dead. He looked steadily at Walsh and said:

"Fight her till she goes down, Jim!"

The assistant to Dr. Downward, Dr. Warder, came up, but the captain waved him away. "I'm still here," Getting said weakly, as his eyes closed and he started to topple off the stool. Engineering Officer Commander McMahon crawled through the rubble and smoke at the wheel house, which had now taken several 8-inch shells. He saw the captain, supported by Coxswain Downs. "Sir," he said, "the engine room copped it bad. I don't think she can last long."

"Do what you can, Mac," Getting replied. *Canberra's* skipper was still dimly conscious—conscious enough to resist the attempts of Downward and Downs to sit him on the deck.

Below, the torpedo had torn a gaping chunk out of the hull, and from it now appeared a weird gray funnel of smoke. Commander McMahon went back down from the bridge to see if there were any chance to keep the ship afloat, at least until all hands had been taken off. The shelling had suddenly ceased and the brassy howl of exploding heavy-caliber ammunition had stopped ringing in the men's ears. Now other ships were catching it across the water.

On deck, flames from the cruiser's two Walrus aircraft cast an eerie reflection on the 4-inch gun decks. The two port guns were smashed and mangled bodies of the crews were lying everywhere like crumpled dolls. Officers and ratings who were still on their feet, after the heavy hand of Mikawa had wrecked their ship, wrestled ammunition which had become heated because the ready-use lockers were ablaze.

As the men fought their way through the holocaust, they grabbed the hot cylinders and 4-inch shells, rushed to the ship's side, and heaved them into the sea. Others battled the flames around fallen shipmates with buckets of water. Still other men were kneeling among the wounded.

The small-arms lockers caught fire now and machine-gun bullets began to set off in bizarre cacophony, a rataplan of death.

On the bridge, Captain Getting was dying. He had given command to Commander Walsh and had stubbornly resisted the attempts of his doctors to stretch him out on the deck. Now, as the little knot of silent men gathered about him, Getting's eyes closed and his head tilted forward until it rested on his white tunic. Twin jets of bright red drained down his neck and gathered in the lower folds just above the collar. The only voice was that of the OOD, muted and choked up, giving orders to a wounded *Canberra* helmsman. There was no other sound.

USS Ralph Talbot off Lahania Roads, Maui.
Seen below, the heavy cruiser USS Astoria.

Capt. Wm. Green-
aman receives the
Legion of Honor
from Asst. Secy.
H. Struve Hensel
in Wash., D. C.

Destroyer Squad, after a raid on Rabaul, maneuvers in a salute to ships sunk near Savo.

**HMAS Canberra, on fire after being mortally hit.
Below, damaged bow of USS Chicago hit by torpedo.**

Adm. Halsey; R. Adm. McCain and Maj. Gen. Vander-grift, USMC. R. Adm. Ghormley; V. Adm. Fletcher.

Lieut. Comdr. Henry Heneberger, gunnery officer aboard the heavy cruiser USS Quincy, seen below.

Above, USS Pattersen. Below, men wounded at Tulagi Island are taken from USS Blue to USS Neville.

Every body was asleep when Mikawa sailed past

Cape Esperance is at left, Savo Island in center.
Below, Savo seen from Guadalcanal in the Solomons.

**Above, R. Adm. Richard Turner, Capt. Samuel Moore.
Below, Com. H. C. Bode, and Adm. Arthur Hepburn.**

All photos courtesy Navy Department

CHAPTER 10

HMAS *Canberra* was out of the war. The first ship in the doomed Southern Force to receive Admiral Mikawa's gunfire and torpedoes, the Australian heavy cruiser had a ten-degree starboard list and was fighting for her life as the exec, Commander James A. Walsh, took over. But Walsh, a stubborn man, was not yet ready to give the order to abandon ship.

Fires were raging in the regulating office flat, after control, and the catapult structures, as well as on the open deck. The 4-inch gun crews and those men at the torpedo nests were either all killed or severely wounded by the concentration of the enemy's main battery fire. Between decks, there were more fires and much smoke.

Commander McMahon, who had left the bridge after speaking with the dying Getting, went back down to his engine rooms. Smoke was funneling up in a dense cloud from "A" boiler room flat, while "B" boiler room flat was a shambles of corpses and machine parts. In the artesian mess, adjacent, on the starboard side, bucket brigades, stepping gingerly over the bodies of fallen seamen, were at work bringing the blaze under control.

McMahon "feared the magazines would go" and passed the word to *Canberra's* acting CO, Commander Walsh. The latter promptly ordered him to flood them down. It was anybody's guess (the list increased another five degrees to starboard) how long the ship would last. Walsh didn't think it would be more than a few minutes; but actually a desperate crew was to keep her alive, *in extremis,* for several hours.

Canberra, McMahon found, was shot through. Reports were streaming to his station below, where a brass speaker tube kept him in touch with the bridge. He had sad news to report after the damage control parties had finished their rounds:

One hit had been scored on "A" barbette port side, upper deck, putting "A" turret out of action for training purposes.

One hit in the torpedomen's mess deck.

Two hits in the foretop mess deck; "B" turret undamaged.

One hit in the stoker's mess deck.

One hit in the plotting office and one hit in the port foremost corner of the forebridge, wiping out the majority of personnel here.

One hit in the foremost end of the main galley, which penetrated to the sick bay.

Torpedo hit in the starboard side, presumably on bulkhead 127 between the boiler rooms.

One hit penetrating through stoker PO's (Petty Officer) mess deck and into "A" fan flat.

"B" boiler room damage unknown at the time of the report.

One hit first motor boat and starboard pompom magazine (from aft).

At least four hits in the 4-inch gun deck.

At least two hits in the torpedo space.

The aircraft and aircraft catapult support both hit.

One hit in the regulating office flat, penetrating to the forward engine room.

One hit in the after director.

One hit in the gunroom flat through the gunnery office.

One hit through the left cabinet, bursting between the guns of "X" turret.

One hit penetrating through the cypher office (immediately forward of the captain's quarters) to the shell handling room.

One hit in the warrant officer's flat.

On receiving this report, Commander Walsh realized the ship couldn't possibly survive the night. He issued orders to slip all gas tanks and fire remaining torpedoes. All magazines were flooded and the wounded men collected on deck. *Canberra* was then closed down amidships in the vain hope that the fire would smother itself. Both cutters and all available rafts were collected on the port side forward, preparatory to lowering. At this juncture the wounded were lowered to the cutters.

In the forward casualty station, already overcrowded, the stretcher cases went first. One of them was Stoker Ray Boys, seventeen. A jagged piece of shrapnel had torn away half of his chest. Dr. Downward, back from the bridge, was binding the youngster's chest with cellophane. To all present this appeared a hopeless case, but the stoker nevertheless remained conscious—sometimes smiling—throughout the operation which was to save his life.

Boys, who was asleep in the recreation space below the bridge when the enemy struck, ran for his life jacket, which was down in sickbay. Until recently he had been a patient on the sick list, and he had inadvertenly left the jacket in this compartment. When the general alarm sounded, Boys raced below—arriving just in time to meet the first of *Chokai's* 8-inch shells. . . .

The experience of Stoker George Yates, nineteen, was similarly ironic. He was about to go on a message for Dr. Downward when the shell struck. As the smoke cleared, Yates dazedly picked himself up and stared at an arm lying on the deck. He screamed:

"Look! Someone's arm has been shot off!"

John Quigley, a ship's butcher, had hit the deck beside Yates when the shell exploded. He reached for his medical kit and ordered:

"Lie down and be quiet, for Chrissakes! It's yours!"

Chief Jon Chipman, the shipwright, was hurrying to his station when the torpedo hit. Concussion flung him down a passageway, end over end, until he rolled to a stop at the door of his working area. Chipman recorded: "After the terrible fight, it was a heaven-sent relief to work. Everywhere through the ship our job was to seek the wounded. The white-clad figures (of the medical party) had fixed to their heads a torch like a miner's lamp. They felt their way up and down ladders and groped through twisted passageways, the torches throwing a weird light that enabled them to find a silent form here and there . . . when they drew near where fires glowed their white suits went rosy, then danced red when near the flames. Minor swift operations were performed, and all manner of treatment was administered to hurt men in all parts of the ship.

"Electricians and artificers and their mates rushed Aldis lamps and torches to every part of the ship, the engineers and staffs frantically trying to put together ruptured watertight compartments. Sliding on greasy plates, half blinded by sudden bursts of smoke, toiling on the slant in water black with oil, these men held the ship together against the hissing inrush of the sea until the wounded could be evacuated."

In "X" shellroom the men had heard the alarm and felt the explosion of a torpedo hitting on the starboard side. Able Seaman Harold Murray, a survivor of this terrible night, noted:

"We waited and waited for word of the ship going into action. None came. It was a rumbling sort of silence through which vibrated what sounded like dull explosions . . . then we began to feel her list over. We were encased in solid steel walls; we had received no orders; no mechanism seemed to be working; we felt like rats in a trap. Again and again we heard a hard, dull noise like a shell hitting the ship.

"We could feel the slow crunching shudders of the ship and the hoarse rumbling noises that we could only guess at. And after what seemed a terribly long time we heard the voice of Petty Officer Hopper calling: 'Hey! Below there! All hands are to come up top.'

"We did, quick and lively. After leaving the shell room we closed the hatch; the compartment was then flooded by orders from the damage control officer. When I reached the upper deck I gazed stupified. The after firing control was ablaze, the 4-inch gun positions were burning and smoking furiously, the guns were silent. Through the smoke and flames men were bending over the wounded. Everybody else appeared to be fighting fires. The superstructure was wrecked; our amphibian plane was in flames, the sea was a lurid glow and the stars (visible now for the first time between squalls) blinked far above a rising cloud of smoke."

Up top, where Commander Walsh was assimilating the bits of information constantly being funneled to him, it was soon apparent that the inevitable could not be postponed. Walsh braced himself to pass the word to abandon ship. It was an order, however, that would not be given for some hours.

CHAPTER 11

THE PATTERSON was the first of the Southern Force warships to go into action. Instantly upon sighting the enemy cruisers, Commander Walker sent a signalman racing to the wing of the bridge. By blinker tube the message was repeated. "Warning! Warning! Strange ships entering harbor!"

It was 1:43 and Japanese torpedoes, fired five minutes earlier, were about to find targets. The destroyer, riding high on the port bow of the *Canberra,* immediately put her wheel hard left to bring main batteries to bear. At the same time gunners fired a starshell and Commander Walker ordered a torpedo spread.

His order went unheard in the roar of the destroyer's gunfire. Even as the main battery let loose and the starshell threw a garish white light on Admiral Mikawa's fast-moving force of ships, enemy gunners concentrated on the *Patterson.* The little ship was hit by return fire which smashed the No. 4 gun, put another gun out of action, and started a fire. The range to Mikawa was 2,000 yards, bearing 70 degrees relative.

Captain Mikeo Hayakawa of the *Chokai* barked the order that turned on the cruiser's powerful searchlight. Now the *Patterson* was bathed in the ghostly beam. But this, instead of worrying her plucky gun crews, made them fighting mad. Several hits were scored on a forward enemy ship. Meanwhile, a party was organized to quell the blaze at No. 4 gun. Commander Walker's guns kept on shooting as long as the enemy ships were in sight. Some 20 rounds of illuminating and 50 rounds of service ammunition was expended in this lopsided but fortunately brief encounter.

On the blazing *Canberra's* starboard bow, the destroyer *Bagley* swung left on orders from Lieutenant Commander George Sinclair. Her speed was 25 knots. Even so, the attack had come so suddenly that the torpedoes couldn't be readied in time for firing. Notwithstanding, in one minute—the elapsed time since the sighting of Mikawa's force—the *Bagley's* crew managed to insert primers and launch a spread of four fish. The estimated range at this point was about 3,000 yards.

Lieutenant John H. Gardiner, USNR, the *Bagley's* JOOD (Junior Officer of the Deck) saw an explosion two minutes after the torpedoes were fired. This was nothing more than a "premature"—a warhead exploding midway on her run. For some unexplained reason, the *Bagley* remained in the area only a moment longer, then sheered off to the northeast at high speed. Later she was to remove *Astoria's* survivors, when the Northern Force entered the action.

Lieutenant Commander A. F. White, the exec of the *Patterson*, was in the secondary conn when his ship was hit in the No. 4 handling room. After organizing repair parties to bring the fire under control, removing the wounded and tossing fiery debris over the side, White remained on deck for most of the night. The *Patterson*, hard hit in this initial moment of battle, was to remove 400 of the *Canberra's* survivors in the next four hours.

E. K. Terrill, SK 3/c (Store Keeper Third Class) fought his way into the burning compartment just as a sailor with clothes completely aflame raced past him toward the railing. Terrill brought the man down with a flying tackle and stripped him. R. C. Willett, BM 2/c (Boatswain's Mate Second Class) likewise had the presence of mind to hurl another human torch to the deck and remove his clothes.

Ralph G. Wilson, CGM (Chief Gunner's Mate) was the burly chief petty officer who, amid the fire and pungent black smoke, organized the remnants of the No. 4 gun crew and took over No. 3 gun. Near him was H. G. Millikan, Sea 2/c (Seaman Second Class) stationed at No. 5 20-millimeter gun. When the shell hit was taken Millikan, hit in both legs and the midriff, stuck at his gun and continued to fire. It was only after the action broke off and when his loader, C. E. Curtis, accidentally jostled him, that Millikan fell to the deck in a pool of blood.

Carrying fourteen casualties, the *Patterson* sheered off after the close of this action, moving northeastward and later returning to take off the *Canberra's* survivors.

Meanwhile, Gunichi Mikawa was licking his chops in anticipation of wreaking new havoc among his foes. On the flag bridge his staff gathered and were busy marking down the graves of the first Allied victims. They had disposed of at least one heavy cruiser and given two destroyers a terrible fright. Now their Long Lance torpedoes were to have another target. It was the *Chicago*, steaming in the Southern Force. She had had three warnings:

At 1:43, two flashes, orange in color, near the surface of the water, were seen near Savo Island. There appeared to be a fire on or near Savo Island at this time.

At 1:43 the first of five aircraft were reported bearing 160 degrees to 170 degrees relative.

At 1:45 the *Canberra* was seen to starboard.

Against an ink-black backdrop, with intermittent lightning flashes ripping across the sky, two objects were sighted by the *Chicago*'s lookouts; then another object. By now Captain Bode, aroused from a deep sleep by the OOD (officer of the deck) raced to the bridge shouting for his 5-inch guns to illuminate with starshell. No sooner was this order executed than a lookout on the starboard wing spotted the phosphorescent wakes from a nest of torpedoes fired by the captain of the *Chokai*.

"Torpedo wakes to starboard!" came the excited cry. And a moment later the *Chicago* was wildly maneuvering to avoid contact. The Long Lances came from 345 degrees, almost dead ahead. On the starboard wing, a cluster of breathless officers and men watched the bubbly wake of the first fish cross about 70 yards ahead of the cruiser's bow. Then the second threaded the black waters about 20 yards ahead. At the foretop, another lookout shouted that the third torpedo was crossing the bow at 300 yards, but the men of the *Chicago* never saw the fish that actually hit them.

(As the cruiser was heeling to port to parallel Long Lance tracks and then back again, flashes of gunfire were seen close aboard bearing 320 relative. And flashes of gunfire were seen from two ships on the starboard bow.) At this moment the torpedo struck the port bow well forward and a column of water deluged the ship from the peak to the No. 1 stack. Captain Bode's gunners sputtered, sucked in their breaths, and let go two four-gun salvos of starshell spearing out from bearing 45 degrees and set for 5,000 yards. Beyond the *Canberra* glutted with fire, was a dark silhouette thought to be a cruiser taking American fire.

Bode's lookouts at this moment saw two destroyers left of *Canberra*, range 2,500 to 4,000 yards. The guns trained around, and as this was happening the first 8-inch shell hit the starboard leg of the *Chicago*'s foremast, showering shrapnel over her topsides. American sailors were falling victims of Mikawa's fury.

The result of the torpedoing was negligible in terms of the *Chicago*'s topside damage. Her foremast was bent so that the Mark 3 antenna would not clear the topmast. The 8-inch gun director would not train. Cable XGE was severed by the enemy's shellfire, putting director No. 1 to an 8-inch gun temporarily out of commission.

But below decks forward, the *Chicago* was in a bad way. Bode sent his damage control officer below and soon the gloomy tidings were telephoned to the bridge:

"The whole damned bow from about three feet above the water line to Frame No. 4 blown away. Wreckage is slewed around to port and trailed along the port side. It's a mess down here, Captain!"

Howard Marshall Hatch, Sea 1/c (Seaman First Class) was topside. Shell splinters tore away one side of his face and scalp. He died at his post.

Chief Boatswain Steve Balint, near Hatch, fell across his gun as a splinter entered his abdomen. Twenty-four other members of the 8-inch gun forward were wounded by *Chokai's* fire. Commander Cecil C. Adell, the exec, hit in the neck, managed to crawl aft to dentist Lieutenant Commander Benjamin Osterting at an emergency medical station set up amidships. The dentist sewed Adell together without anesthesia. Down below, in the *Chicago*'s operating room, young Arthur Cornelius Reid, a seaman, was being prepared for the amputation of his left leg.

As the cruiser's guns trained around, a ship ahead—believed to be the *Patterson*—illuminated with searchlight two targets, Mikawa's destroyer and flagship. Whereupon the port battery opened fire at 7,200 yards. Two hits by the tin can were observed. Bode's gunners, on the other hand, were unable to get a set-up on the enemy for lack of starshells, and this target was lost. Another Jap shell now fell on the *Chicago,* and the 5.25-inch No. 1 gun was damaged by fragments.

About the *Chicago*'s catapults, too, the cruiser was in a bad way. Plane No. 4, bureau No. 0388, was ablaze. A large shell fragment had struck the CO_2 bottle, exploding and tearing away the diagonal main fuselage strength members between stations No. 1 and No. 2 on the right side of the aircraft. Fire had crumpled the entire right side before this blaze was brought under control. All of the *Chicago*'s aircraft, including the one on loan from the *Portland,* sustained some damage.

About the No. 3 gun, wounded men crawled toward the emergency medical station. An enemy projectile had struck the gun shield between two 5-inch guns, penetrated the shield, and apparently detonated a foot or two behind it. The result was a thorough drenching of the area in shrapnel.

At 1:50 a frustrated Captain Bode ordered the *Chicago's* searchlights snapped on. His 44 starshells were expended. Even as he sprinted to the port wing, Nos. 2 and 4 lights were sweeping the area to port. Across the black waters were two destroyers, one frantically zigzagging and the other steaming away at high speed. Both ships were identified as friendly. In disgust, Bode ordered the lights turned off.

"Slowed to twelve knots at 1:54," he recorded. "Withdrew for Lengo Channel. All firing ceased, no ships visible."

Thus, licking her wounds, the cruiser steamed off to the westward—Mikawa moved to the northeast.

But the sin of omission that was to plague Howard Bode the rest of his short life was his failure to warn the Northern Force. A fiery maelstrom was about to be visited upon these warships and they had no knowledge of it whatever.

The *Vincennes, Quincy* and *Astoria,* with destroyers *Helm* and *Wilson* screening ahead, were at the time approaching the southeastern corner of the square that they patrolled. Riding at ten knots, these ships saw only the black of night until they encountered Admiral Mikawa's searchlights and felt the sting of his guns. On the Japanese ships there was a brief moment for quiet elation. All hands now felt "supremely confident." The long years of night-vision gunnery practice were paying dividends—as they would again, in exactly three minutes.

At 1:44 the flagship's wheel was put over hard left to bearing 68 degrees. Somehow this maneuver went awry, and as a consequence the Japanese task force split in two—the left column *Chokai, Aoba, Kako* and *Kinugasa* in formation to the east of *Yubari, Tenyru* and *Furutaka.* Mikawa was not distressed, even by a narrowly averted collision of two ships. It was no moment for reproving his men. They had tasted the Allied turkey and were about to eat it, bones and all.

CHAPTER 12

HELL WAS about to break loose. Admiral Mikawa's Tokyo Express was roaring down on fresh targets to the northeast of Savo Island. Very quickly now, *Chokai's* powerful 36-inch searchlights would illuminate the heavy cruiser *Astoria*, aftermost ship in the Northern Force, and sharp-eyed Orientals would work her over with a concentration of main battery fire.

On the *Astoria's* bridge, Lieutenant Commander James R. Topper, thirty-four, damage control officer acting as supervisor of the watch, scanned the black night uneasily. An enemy attack was expected. A troubled calm had descended since shortly after midnight, when the captain had slipped into his emergency cabin for a nap. Submarine contacts had been frequent these two days in the Solomons, but as the second hour of the midwatch steadily drew to a close there were no outward manifestations of trouble. Nine men stood watch with Topper.

Captain William G. Greenman, fifty-four, a kindly, soft-spoken man from Watertown, New York, ran a "happy ship."

"Patrolling at ten knots. Nothing to report," the quartermaster's log read. The ship was steaming on intercardinal courses forming a square whose sides were five miles each. The course was normally changed on the hour and half hour to the right 90 degrees.

"Sea smooth, surface visibility fair. Ceiling down about 1,500 feet, except around Savo Island, which is enclosed by haze," the log also noted. The heavy cruiser, 9,950 tons, was at Condition II, with four of her seven boilers on the line and the rest shut down but still warm.

Greenman (Annapolis '12), an enthusiastic athlete, had been a member of the crew during his midshipman years, and the captain of his first-year class. He had come up through the line and was still another who was ready for flag rank, but who would attain only the rank of commodore in retirement after Savo. Bill Greenman would fight gamely tonight, however confused this fight might appear in retrospect. He had come aboard the *Astoria* from a staff job with Commander Destroyers, Atlantic Fleet, only three months before—to a ship which had distinguished herself as part of the screening force at Coral Sea and Midway. He knew he was biting off a mouthful.

The Northern Force—*Vincennes, Quincy* and *Astoria*, in column in that order, with destroyers *Wilson* and *Helm* on the starboard and port bow respectively—was patrolling the area between Savo Island and the western end of Florida Island. Lieutenant Commander Topper, relieving Lieutenant Commander John A. Hayes, the engineering officer, had taken over at 11:45. It had thus far been a quiet, if not down-right soporific, watch on the bridge.

At 1:44 (while Mikawa was polishing off Captain Bode's Southern Force) Topper noticed gunfire on Florida Island. He observed to Lieutenant N. A. Burkey that "the Marines are having a hell of a time on the islands tonight." So they were.

A moment later two faint explosions were felt on the bridge and Topper, who evidently hadn't heard the warning screamed by a frantic destroyer captain over the TBS that strange ships were entering the harbor, believed these explosions to be depth charges dropped by one of the tin cans in the anchorage area. Actually they were Japanese torpedoes reaching the end of their run after being fired at *Chicago* and exploding. A few minutes passed. Mikawa was ready to strike again, and things began to happen.

"Someone ran in from the port wing of the bridge reporting starshells on the port quarter," Topper notes. "I ran to the port door of the pilot house and aft and directed the officer of the deck (Burkey) to call the captain and stand-by the general alarm."

Burkey sprinted for the door between the house and Captain Greenman's cabin. The four-striper, who had gone to bed in his clothes, awoke from a deep sleep. Lieutenant Commander William H. Truesdell, the gunnery officer, heard the report, "Starshells astern!" and immediately went outside the control station to the sky control station. There "Guns" saw the four "stars," which appeared to him as aircraft flares, not starshells. He ordered all stations alert and went to tell Commander Topper to sound the general alarm. Then Truesdell amended this by telling the bridge to sound general quarters. To him, flares meant enemy action. As the gunnery officer was hurrying to the control station, Mikawa's gunners commenced firing. The first salvos were short and ahead.

In the wheel house R. A. Radke, QM 2/c (Quartermaster Second Class) had been standing at the general alarm switch. He saw a ship on the *Astoria's* bow open fire, and promptly jerked the alarm without orders. Actually Topper had only yelled, "Stand by to sound general alarm!" but the deed—and a good one it was—was already done. The bell was ringing as "Guns" gave the order to commence firing. I was 1:52 when six 8-inch guns blasted out at the *Chokai*.

Topper, on the port wing, saw no ship. He turned and started for the house as a second salvo roared out. By now the captain was in the house asking Topper:

"Who sounded the general alarm? Who gave the order to commence firing?"

To say the least, it was an awkward moment for Greenman of the *Astoria*. Topper, caught in a maze of confusion, started to reply, but the commanding officer said quickly:

"Topper, I think we are firing on our own ships. Let's not get excited and act too hastily. Cease firing!"

The order went out and the guns fell silent. Topper turned to Captain Greenman and very quickly explained that he had given neither the order to sound the general alarm nor the one to commence firing. Adding zest to his explanation, Topper said that he believed "we were firing on our own ships." From main battery control at this juncture came the word that *Astoria* was firing on *recognized* Japanese cruisers! Now someone from the port wing ran in and reported that a searchlight was lighting warships to port and that these ships *appeared* to be firing at them from out on the horizon!

But the comedy of errors was about to come to a screeching halt. As Captain Greenman and Lieutenant Commander Topper were debating what all this meant in terms of the *Astoria,* the word was flashed over the telephone and relayed by a sailor, who said to Greenman:

"Mr. Truesdell said for God's sake give the word to commence firing!"

Over the TBS at this moment came word from the *Vincennes* that speed had been upped to fifteen knots—but nothing more! The commanding officer shook his groggy head in bewilderment. Reports were streaming in from the port wing that ships were firing on them from that side. Greenman, a little wistfully, remarked:

"Whether they're our ships or not, we will have to stop them." Then he ordered: "Commence firing!"

Now Greenman directed Topper to go to his GQ station which was central control. At this time the OOD was ordered to ring up all engines ahead and left full rudder. The *Quincy*, next ship in line, bore watching in this collision-inspiring melee.

Thus far, the enemy had fired four salvos—all of them short—but the discussion on the bridge had given him time to correct his aim and now the shells began to fall on target. His fifth salvo hit amidships. It had come from the Japanese flagship, Admiral Mikawa directing. One of the first hits was in Battle Two, secondary control. Commander Frank E. Shoup, the exec, had awakened instantly on the ringing of general quarters, thrown his clothes over his pajamas and run back to his battle station. John U. Walker, QM 2/c, was the only man present.

Shoup stepped out on the starboard side to see what the fuss was about. He saw nothing. Next he walked to the machine-gun platform on the port quarter "to get an unobstructed view." He did. As Shoup went out the door and leaned over the splinter shield, an enemy shell came aboard. Shoup threw up his hands to cover his eyes, and it was a good thing that he reacted instinctively. The shell exploded nearby and fragments rained over the immediate area, burning his hands and face and, for a few moments, blinding him. The shell had penetrated the hangar bulkhead directly under Shoup's battle station. In a moment the cruiser's catapult planes were ablaze, a veritable bonfire below him.

Now Turret 3 had lost power and the *Astoria* had only the punch of Turrets 1 and 2. It was not nearly enough, as Mikawa's gunners had a fine burning target and the range was well down to 6,000 yards. In addition, the *Chokai's* searchlights were now in operation. Enemy gunners poured out their shells with a vengeance as the piercing beams of light revealed three heavy cruisers steaming in formation, with the faint outlines of the screening destroyers beyond them. As salvo after salvo crept inexorably toward the killing range, huge geysers of water leaped up in the blackness between the two forces. Now shells were seen to be hitting on targets.

On the *Astoria*, the closest ship, there were fires on deck, up forward and at the hangar. No. 1 gun was put out of action almost immediately, killing all hands in the chamber and upper powder rooms.

In the central station, Topper had a narrow squeak with eternity. Within a minute after he'd arrived at his battle station this room was a smoke-filled caldron. Topper noted: "Large pieces of hot sparking metal, burning rubber and debris dropped on deck. . . . A shell exploded directly above us. Halligan (T. C. Halligan, Sea 1/c) grabbed the CO_2 fire extinguisher and played it on the debris."

Nevertheless, central station was able to stay in operation a while longer. On the bridge, Captain Howard Greenman saw his ship approaching the *Quincy's* line of fire (the three cruisers were blazing amidships now as salvos began to fall with sickening regularity), and he promptly ordered right standard rudder to permit her to draw ahead.

The cruiser shifted her main battery fire to starboard. At this moment the *Astoria's* bridge was hit just forward of the door leading to the pilot house. Shrapnel sprayed the compartment, killing, among others, Quartermaster First Class R. Williams, and severely wounding Boatswain's Mate First Class J. Young. The latter staggered to his feet, pushed away the dead helmsman, and took the wheel. Captain Greenman was unhurt.

Suddenly the *Quincy* appeared on the port bow, "heading across at considerable speed. She was on fire from stem to stern. It looked as if we would hit her."

Greenman ran out to the wing and from there yelled, "Left rudder! Hard left rudder!"

As the ships passed clear of each other, the wheel was brought back amidships and the violent heeling stopped. But Helmsman Young couldn't tell where his ship was heading. The binnacle light was out and he had no way of knowing if the instrument were working.

Greenman called the communications deck and ordered Turret 2 to train on a searchlight abaft the port beam. Young, with one arm hanging limp and blood cascading into his dungarees, collapsed at the wheel. Quartermaster Second Class R. A. Radke, who was attending the wounded, saw Young fall and lunged for the wheel.

"I think we're on 185 degrees, Radke," Young whispered. "Stay with it—"

Meanwhile, an 8-inch shell had ploughed through *Astoria's* bridge and exploded in the chart house, killing most of the personnel. Fires immediately broke out and the pungent black smoke from the hit itself was soon seeping into the blood-drenched wheel house.

Yeoman Second Class W. F. Putnam was the telephone talker on the open bridge when the action commenced. Outside, Putnam had a clear view of the *Quincy* crossing the *Astoria*'s bow, while blazing about her superstructure and well deck. Beside him was Ensign T. Ferneding, the signal officer of the watch.

"Holy smokes, look at that!" Ferneding gulped. By the time Young could mutter a pithy comment, the signal officer was hit by a piece of flying shrapnel and slowly sagged to his knees. Putnam ripped off his headphones, dragged the officer under the shelter of the bridge, and asked if he could do anything else.

"Gimme a cigarette," Ferneding croaked. Putnam did, then rushed back to the wing.

When he returned, the ship had moved clear of the *Quincy*. On the signal bridge, Lieutenant N. A. Burkey was standing at his battle station. The gun deck was already in flames as a result of direct hits, and the 5-inch ready boxes had begun to explode with a terrible racket. On the boat deck the ship's motor launches, holed and smashed to kindling, had started to burn. Livid tongues of flame danced about the bodies of Burkey's shipmates.

In the engine rooms the black gang was catching hell. Lieutenant Commander John D. Hayes, the engineering officer, who had been on the bridge as supervisor prior to Topper, roamed from fireroom to fireroom, where dead and dying men littered the decks.

When the action opened Hayes had been sound asleep in his quarters. He had never heard general quarters go off, and had it not been for messenger Motor Machinist First Class J. Bengal, who came down and shook him into consciousness, Hayes might well have remained in the sack until too late.

"Mr. Hayes," Bengal snapped. "You're wanted down below. The shells have begun to fall."

Hayes staggered out of bed, dressed and proceeded to the forward engine room, where he remained until all steam was lost.

In main radio, Lieutenant George Baker was having a time of it. Baker, in the coding room when this compartment was hit, crawled over bloody bodies when the smoke of the explosion had cleared and, with Pay Clerk B. Q. Swinson, set about removing the wounded. A shell had penetrated the armored door and exploded in the comm office, and another had sliced through the armored bulkhead and exploded in Radio 1. Most of the men who had been on watch here were killed outright. And communications equipment—all of it—was wrecked. Radio 2 was finished off by Gunichi Mikawa in the same fashion.

But, everything considered, the gunnery department of the *Astoria* had acquitted itself well. Though it had started late, it was managing to squeeze out the last few rounds through two operative turrets, Nos. 2 and 3. In all, 62 rounds of 8-inch ammunition would be expended. Truesdell's 5-inch port battery would hammer out 28 rounds, his starboard battery 31 rounds; twelve of his 20-millimeter guns would send 270 rounds at the enemy, and his 1.1 mounts (four of them) would fire 778 rounds.

Lieutenant D. R. Marzatta was in the plotting room when heavy-caliber fire smashed the compartment. When the flash of the explosion had died away, the room was enveloped in pungent black smoke, and the stench of cordite filled the air.

"Request permission to secure chart room. We got it. Impossible to breathe in here," Marzatta wheezed to central control.

"Get your gas mask on and stay put," the reply came back. The few survivors did as ordered.

"There were no signs of fear or panic among the men," Marzatta noted. "After donning gas masks we had to shout through them in order to be heard over the phones, but communications were maintained as before."

Captain Greenman, hit 11 times by shrapnel, was still on his feet as the battle moved away from the flaming *Astoria* and his ship began to die. He hailed Lieutenant Commander Walter B. Davidson, who was climbing on Turret 2 to direct fire visually, now that FC radar was smashed and communications were out. Davidson complied by directing a hit on Mikawa's gun-roaring cruiser. It was small compensation for the pain of defeat.

CHAPTER 13

A COMMUNICATIONS failure between bridge and gunnery control stations helped put the *Quincy,* next ahead of the *Astoria,* into a watery grave 500 fathoms deep in Savo Sound.

Simultaneously with the TBS warning from *Patterson* that strange ships were entering the harbor, a messenger was sent to wake the commanding officer. About this time general quarters was sounded. In the confusion somebody forgot to tell the gunnery control station.

Captain Samuel N. Moore, fifty-one, tumbled out of bed in his emergency cabin and rushed to the bridge. He was just in time to see starshells falling over the sound. Beside him, binoculars raised, Lieutenant (jg) C. P. Clarke, Jr. was staring at three silhouettes which appeared to be rounding the southern end of Savo Island.

Clarke focused on the leading ship and tensed. It had three turrets forward, the middle one higher than the others. Lieutenant Commander Edward E. Billings, supervisor of the watch, hurried out as Clarke announced: "They're not our ships, Captain!"

Moore was not so positive.

On the control platform, Lieutenant John D. Andrew was on watch. He was the ship's assistant gunnery officer. To him the starshells meant nothing more than American ships defending the transports against aircraft. Possibly, he thought, they were trying to pinpoint the location of a plane which had been buzzing around for the last hour.

The general alarm startled and confused him. Wasn't control supposed to be informed if the enemy had appeared? Who had sounded the alarm, and why? Had the enemy actually appeared? Andrew could only guess.

But this moment of speculation quickly ended as the *Aoba's* searchlights flicked on and piercing white beams of light probed the darkness of the sound. Shells began to fall almost at the same instant. Captain Morre was still doubtful (he never saw the strange silhouettes) but he shouted:

"Fire on the searchlights!"

The illumination came from abaft the port beam, distant about 8,500 yards.

Already at his battle station, Andrew greeted Lieutenant Commander H. B. Heneberger as the latter stormed into the control station. What little information Andrew possessed at this time was hastily imparted to "Guns." Heneberger, too, didn't get it. Was it some kind of drill? But as the Condition II crew rushed out and the battle station crew took over, Japanese shells began to hurtle through the night. The first salvos fell short. Then the searchlights fell squarely on the three American heavy cruisers, and in the 1.1-inch mounts the first shell came aboard.

Moments later the plot light came on and a nine-gun salvo roared out from Quincy's turrets. Then another. The range was down to 8,000 yards, calculated speed fifteen knots. On the bridge Captain Moore, two months removed from a staff job in the Division of Naval Intelligence, had grave misgivings about this action. He decided that he wanted the recognition lights turned on, despite the protestations of his junior officers.

At this time the *Vincennes* ordered a course change and the Quincy's helmsman, on orders from the OOD, swung the wheel hard over to avoid a collision with the leading ship in the Northern Force. Even as he was doing this, Japanese gunners got the range and turned one of the Quincy's catapult jobs into a bonfire. There was no need for searchlights now, nor any doubt in Moore's mind as to the identity of these strangers. The falling salvos were eloquent calling cards.

The *Quincy,* caught in a crossfire between the *Chokai* group and the *Furutaka* group, was soon to be on her way to the bottom of Savo Sound.

"Word was received in control forward from the bridge that the ship was changing course to starboard . . . . The bearing was shifting rapidly to port," Heneberger records. "Control of the main battery was shifted to Director 2 in order to fire Turret 3 since Director 1 would no longer bear. At this time Turret 3 reported being hit and jammed in train."

The *Quincy,* 9,375 tons, began to die.

"From the group of three enemy ships," Toshikazau Ohmae, on the bridge of the *Chokai,* notes, "The center one bore out and down on us as if intending to ram. Though her entire hull from midships aft was enveloped in flames, her forward guns

were firing with great spirit. She was a brave ship, manned by
brave men."

From this moment the *Quincy*, fresh from Atlantic convoy
duty, where a shot was seldom fired in anger, was repeatedly
hit by large and small caliber shells. Enemy fire raked her
from stem to stern. On her fantail No. 3 mount of the 1.1,
desperate men were bringing under control the holocaust
which had been started by the first shell. The after 1.1 clipping
room was flooded against the likelihood of an explosion. Main
pressure for the hoses failed at this point, while up forward
the 1.1 clipping room was hit and blazing. Flames enveloped
control forward.

There were dead men lying in the 20-millimeter mounts.
Both clipping rooms, fore and aft, had been hit and a series of
seemingly unending explosions rocked the ship.

On the starboard AA battery the word was received from
the bridge shattered the wheel house. Steering was lost. Com-
Three salvos belched out before these guns were silenced. That
night, riddled with tracers and screaming shells, was to be the
last for the men on the Quincy's bridge. The first hit taken by
the bridge shattered the wheel house. Steering was lost. Commander William C. Gray, the executive officer; Lieutenant
Commander Edward C. Metcalfe, the navigator; Lieutenant
Commander Raymond H. Tuttle, the damage control officer;
several telephone talkers and the helmsman were killed outright. Captain Moore and one or two other officers and enlisted
men were mortally wounded. Moore crawled to a phone and
gasped:

"We're going down between them—give them hell!"

Two six-gun salvos spat at Mikawa from Turrets 1 and 2.
Then Turret 2 exploded as a direct hit smashed through walls
of thick steel. On the signal bridge the flag bags went up with
a tremendous whoosh and the stench of burned flesh wafted on
the night air. Above the dying *Quincy* the sky was cherry red,
laced around the flaming ship by strings of garish red-and-
white tracers.

Lieutenant Andrew climbed down from the control platform (all communications were now out) to get instructions
from Captain Moore and "to inform him of the damage to the
battery."

As Andrew reached the bridge level, he saw a sight he
would never forget:

"I found it in a shambles of dead bodies, with only three or
four people still standing. In the pilot house itself the only

person standing was the signalman at the wheel, who was vainly endeavoring to check the ship's swing to starboard and bring her to port." Andrew stepped over the bloody corpses and moved to the side of the signalman. Meanwhile, the rear of the compartment was burning furiously and the decks were beginning to slant to port.

"On questioning him," Andrew said, "I found out that the captain, who was at this time lying near the wheel, had instructed him to beach the ship and he was trying to head for Savo Island, distant some four miles on the port quarter . . . . At this instant the captain straightened up and fell back, apparently dead, without having uttered any sound other than a moan."

Andrew quickly left the bridge and returned to Heneberger on the control platform. By now there was nothing to control. The radar antennae had been clipped, all power and telephone systems were out, fires were leaping up from the bridge. Flames swept the powder hoists in Turret 3, which had become jammed in train and was rocketing along the trays, throwing up blinding tongues of fire. Few who had entered this room at the beginning of the battle crawled out when it was over.

Turret 2 was beyond salvation—all hands were dead. In the booth and on the shell deck of Turret 2, large caliber hits had rocketed in and the officer in charge had ordered the sprinkler system turned on for fear that the powder room would blow. Down in Turret 1 (and 2 while it was still in existence) the gun crews knew of the Japanese split formation—probably not long after Mikawa himself did. These turrets had been repeatedly hit on both sides throughout the engagement.

Quincy fought to the end. One of her turrets had spewed out an 8-inch shell which smashed into the operations room of *Chokai*, abaft the bridge, and wrecked the No. 1 turret. Had this shell fallen a few yards forward, Admiral Mikawa and his staff would have joined their ancestors. It might even have changed the outcome of the battle. A leaderless task force in enemy waters? At this point, anything was possible.

The scene at both 5-inch AA Batteries resembled the interior of a slaughterhouse. Sprawled grotesquely over their guns, lying crumpled in bloody, shapeless heaps, were the crews of guns Nos. 6 and 8. Shrapnel had mowed down all hands. They were luckier on guns Nos. 2 and 4—a few men crawled away. On No. 4 gun the shells in the fuse pots were hit. The result was a deadly Roman-candle effect that killed all hands on the left side of the gun. The ready boxes on guns Nos. 1 and 5 exploded, and smoke from this, along with smoke drifting back from the superstructure, blinded those men who were still alive and fighting the batteries.

Mikawa had brought his fight in as close as 2,000 yards. His ships had hammered the *Quincy* into a fiery scrap heap. Few ships in history had taken this kind of a beating; fewer still had gone down shooting off their weapons. But the *Quincy* did. Even as she began to admit the waters of Savo Sound, the roar of an isolated 5-inch gun sundered the night.

Lieutenant W. A. Hall Jr., the ship's dentist, himself badly wounded, crawled around the 5-inch gun deck trying to assist others. Finding his pharmacist's mate bleeding to death from the loss of a leg under a gun mount, he dragged the half-conscious man to a bulkhead. Hall grabbed the stump and held it to his stomach in an effort to staunch the flow of blood.

Radio I went out of business early in the fight. At about the time that Turret 2 and the forward 20-millimeter mounts were hit, a shell crashed into the communications office, putting the FC radar out of commission. Fire broke out and communications went dead. Lieutenant Roland Rieve, radar officer, went up to the next deck to the SC Radar in Radar I. There was no Radar I any more—just small fires and debris. The transmitter was shattered and pieces were scattered about the deck. Lieutenant Earl E. Ordway, radio officer, tucked the secret codes into the ship's safe. Smoke and flames drove the survivors topside.

When water pressure failed, fire-fighting parties in No. 2 messhall found themselves trapped. For one thing, it was impossible to reach "R" Division compartments where life jackets were stored; for another, it was almost pitch black, because of the power failure and the thick smoke pouring up from below. This compartment was abandoned as the water waned, and the fire fighters retreated to the open deck, where there were other jackets—those which hadn't burned up in the inferno roaring topside.

Lieutenant Commander Eugene E. Elmore, engineering officer, had nothing to offer but communicationless death traps to his black gang if they stayed below and powered the *Quincy*. Nevertheless they stayed, despite the cases of smoke poisoning and later the casualties from Mikawa's last hits. There was no let-up.

Elmore, about ten minutes before the ship lost power, sent a messenger topside to tell Captain Moore that his ship would have to stop. Two hits had been scored on the No. 1 fireroom. The emergency feed pump was gone and fuel suction had been lost. Tubes in No. 2 boiler, rocked by concussion, had burst. At Frame 53 the emergency pump was shattered by a hit forward.

In the Nos. 2, 3 and 4 firerooms blowers had stopped, water pressure had stopped, and the port bulkhead spouted a leak that was anything but comforting to the men in the bowels of the ship. Steam pressure dropped rapidly. In No. 4, the men thought they took a torpedo hit (back aft they felt the explosion too and it sounded to them like a torpedo). In this room, smoke filled and bright with flames, nearly all perished.

Lieutenant Commander Heneberger, senior surviving officer, who was still on the control platform, felt the deck canting forward. He had the sad report from his assistant, Topper. There was no way remaining of formally announcing, "Abandon ship!" All hands would simply lay below to the railing and prepare to leave.

Overhead, the covering of night was bright orange from the eerie reflection of the *Quincy*'s fires, and black around the edges. The men went overboard to floater nets and rafts being held to the side.

"All hands abandoned ship in an orderly manner when so directed," Heneberger records. *Quincy* sank bow first, rolling to port in a welter of hissing steam and internal explosions. It was 2:35 A.M.

CHAPTER 14

THE *Vincennes,* leader of the Northern Force of cruisers, and the last ship to be fired on by Admiral Mikawa, ran out of luck early in the battle. Eighteen minutes after the battle started she was a fiery wreck.

Captain Frederick L. Riefkohl—"Fearless Freddie" to his colleagues—fought his ship bravely to the end. A fiery derelict utterly unable to shoot off a gun, she was pounded to death by a hailstorm of hammer blows. *Vincennes* never had a chance.

Riefkohl, fifty-one, was aware that the enemy was sending down "three cruisers, three destroyers, and two seaplane tenders," and that an attack was expected before daybreak. He was sensitive to the responsibility of the Northern Force, which he commanded. At a conference on the bridge long before the battle, Riefkohl had stressed the importance of vigilance to his officers (and they to the crew), and had even written something to that effect in his night orders.

At 12:50 A.M., as Captain Riefkohl strode the bridge of the *Vincennes* for the last time in 21 hours, he told Commander W. E. A. Mullen, the executive officer—his relief—to "wake me if anything unusual happens." Prophetic words. Soon after the watch settled down for what seemed at first like another dreary night, "Fearless Freddie" retired to his emergency cabin. Lieutenant Commander Cleaveland D. Miller was OOD, and Lieutenant Commander R. R. Craighill was gunnery officer of the watch.

The first 80 minutes passed quietly. At 1:20 A.M. Miller ordered a course change on the TBS. *Vincennes,* leading the *Quincy* by 600 yards, and the *Astoria* by 1,200 yards, with destroyers *Helm* and *Wilson* forward as the anti-submarine screen, swung her wheel to 315 degrees. The ship was at Condition II, with two guns manned and fully loaded in each turret. AA Batteries were fully manned.

The commanding officer of the cruiser had come up through the line. He had shown a distinct preference for destroyer

103

duty (*Smith Thompson; Corry;* Desron 3) and was obviously a man who didn't shy from action. As a lieutenant (jg) in command of the Armed Guard aboard USMS *Philadelphia,* Riefkohl, twenty-eight, had ridden the North Atlantic convoy lanes with a "hot gun crew." The Navy Cross (the medal held lower designation in those days) was awarded to "Captain Riefkohl" for an action taken on board the mine sweeper on August 2, 1917:

> "For distinguished service in the line of his pro-fession as Commander of the Armed Guard ... and in an engagement with an enemy submarine. A peri-scope was sighted and then a torpedo, which passed under the stern of the ship. A shot was fired which struck close to the submarine as it disappeared."

"Vinny Maru" was every bit as distinguished as her master. Only six years old (commissioned on May 21, 1936 at a cost of $22,000,000) the 9,400-ton *Vincennes* and two destroyers soon joined the Atlantic Fleet. On her first mission the cruiser and two destroyers sped to neutral Lisbon to protect American interests. In those days the United States was short of gold and the *Vincennes,* her holds laden with the stuff, purchased from France, was chosen to make the shipment. She had spent the early part of the war on the North Atlantic convoy lanes, but had come through the canal in time for the battles of Coral Sea and Midway. Nearly 600 feet long and fast (36 knots), this sleep-fighting machine was manned by a crew of approxi-mately 1,000 officers and men. Now one of them, Lieutenant Commander Craighill, quite accidentally was about to bring her closer to action.

"Object broad on the port bow!" a lookout shouted.

Craighill, relieving Commander R. L. Adams, searched the entire area from the port beam forward with binoculars, but saw nothing. A rain squall was hovering over the corner of Savo Island and Craighill, after making another sweep, low-ered the glasses.

"Let me know if you see it again," he said uneasily. Craig-hill swept around through 360 degrees, but there was nothing. On the bridge, port wingtip lookouts continued to peer hard at the corner of Savo Island. For the next 23 minutes nothing happened.

At 1:43 Craighill was back on the platform for another check of the horizon. A flash "which might have been gunfire, lighted the sky for an instant," at the exact moment that

"Guns" was swinging his glasses fromt he port beam to the quarter. Now, quickly, four pairs of binoculars swiveled around to the spot. The light died out. A few seconds later four starshells burst broad on the port quarter "distant about eight miles." This was enough for Craighill. He telephoned the bridge.

"Four starshells on the port quarter!"

OOD Miller turned to the messenger. "Call the captain!"

There was a sudden great display of light off to the southeast, and the silhouettes of Bode's Southern Force were seen framed in the center. (Mikawa was working with torpedo and gunfire at this moment, a job that would take his men exactly six minutes!) Captain Riefkohl, rubbing the sleep out of his eyes, appeared at once. Commander Mullen filled the captain in on events. One of the ships looked to be of the Australia class.

"Sound the general alarm!" Riefkohl ordered.

As the crews rushed to their battle stations, he swung his binoculars to another starshell burst to the southeast. Lieutenant Commander R. L. Adams, ship's gunnery officer, had been the gunnery officer on the eight-to-twelve. Craighill had relieved him for the midnight watch but, instead of going down to his cabin, Adams had laid down on the sky control platform and gone to sleep. When the string of starshells began falling, Adams awakened. He bolted upright in time to see fireworks over Lunga Point. His first reaction was that "some ship was firing at shore installations." In the next moment Adams saw an exchange of gunfire coming from the right and left under the illumination. A telephone report went down to the bridge. Simultaneously, Riefkohl sounded the alarm.

Meanwhile, Adams ordered "Action port!" to the AA batteries and charged into the control station shouting to train out the main battery. Craighill, his assistant, ordered a starshell charge and departed on the double for his battle station at sky control.

Riefkohl and Mullen, standing on the open bridge, speculated on the significance of the gunfire. What did all this mean to the Northern Force? Riefkohl didn't know for sure, but he was ready to wager it was some kind of a ruse to draw off the *Vincennes* group while the enemy slipped through his sector. "If enemy fire had been sighted I expected Australia group would illuminate and engage them," he opined. But no illumination followed. "I signaled fifteen knots to the group and decided to hold my course temporarily." Two underwater explosions were felt in *Vincennes,* but, again, Riefkohl judged this to be nothing!

Speed of the Northern Group was increased from ten to fifteen knots. (Mikawa had cleaned up the Southern Force. It was 1:49, just six minutes after the Tokyo Express was seen by destroyer *Patterson.*)

Commander Mullen now departed for Battery 2, his battle station, and Riefkohl was alone in his bewilderment. Not for long, however. In exactly one minute, three searchlights bearing 205 degrees were seen by all hands. Quickly they found the *Vincennes* group. Riefkohl, who was about to receive the shock of his life, issued orders over the TBS that the lights be turned off!

Mikawa acknowledged by sweeping in closer at 34 knots, his three spots playing on the doomed American cruisers.

In gunnery control, Adams trained the main battery on the nearest light and awaited the order to commence firing. He didn't have long to wait. The first salvo from *Kako* came screaming down a moment later, 500 yards short. *Vincennes* promptly opened fire with a full 8-inch salvo at a radar range of 8,250 yards. Her second salvo, fired at the moment that the enemy force was shooting off its second salvo, hit *Kinugasa* (1 killed). As shells began to fall on *Vincennes,* bad luck made itself apparent.

A salvo of 5-inch gunfire fell on the cruiser's well deck and started a conflagration in that area. Aircraft sitting on hangars blew up with a frightening roar, illuminating *Vincennes* so that Mikawa no longer had need of his searchlights.

Mullen chose this moment to be going to his battle station. He was part way down a ladder as one salvo hit in the movie booth and another on the well deck. Flames soared up with devastating ease as aviation gas burst into a roaring bonfire. Mullen emerged on deck in time to see another shell (8-inch) hitting the hangar, penetrating, and falling on the other side of the vessel about 300 yards away. Organizing fire-fighting crews, Mullen spent the next few minutes getting the pumps to operate. Actually the fire was in the process of being controlled when another shell hit on and smashed the water main risers. Pressure fell quickly. *Vincennes* was allowed to die in her consuming flames.

While this was happening on the main deck, Captain Riefkohl was having his troubles: "Speed was increased to 20 knots and a turn made to left with a view of closing with the enemy and continuing around on a reverse course if he stood in toward the transport area. Attempts to signal increase in speed failed due to loss of intership communications facilities (TBS) after the bridge was hit. . . . One 5-inch shell struck the port side of the bridge, killing the communications officer. Fragments entered the pilot house, killing or seriously wounding several men."

Riefkohl nevertheless made his turn and *Astoria* and *Quincy* followed. Greenman and Moore were old hands at the ancient destroyer game of "follow the leader" tactics, and when they saw the *Vincennes* coming around they did the same. Now the hammer blows began to fall from two sides. The after fire control director was blown overboard. Below the bridge, the 5-inch gun platforms were smashed and burning. The wounded lay silently with the dead, unable to be heard over the deafening roar of gunfire. Power failed in the turrets, but gunfire continued because of local control. The signal bags lying about the decks ignited and more flames soared into the night sky.

Hits thundered in on the port 5-inch ammunition passageway, warrant officers' country and sick bay. Dr. Blackwood, the senior medical officer, was operating by battle lamp, attempting to sew a mess attendant's severed jaw. As a shell hit, the surgeon fell across the operating table. The startled patient leaped off the table, holding his jaw with his hands, and raced out.

On the bridge, when steering control was lost, Captain Riefkohl shifted to the steering engine room, using the white pointer. Batt 2 took a direct hit. Warrant Machinist S. J. Nemeth, in charge of a crew passing ammunition through No. 7 hoist, sent up five rounds when his hoist went dead. He promptly sent an electrician's mate to the compartment above to check the fuse in the hoist panel. Coming back in two minutes, the man reported that the fuse was all right. Nemeth tried the hoist again. It still didn't work. Assistant Pay Clerk James L. Willness was in main radio when the action opened. Here radar went out first, then radio transmitters, then intership communications, in that order.

"*Quincy* was observed on fire aft, on our port hand. *Astoria* was not seen. *Helm* and *Wilson* were ahead on the starboard hand when we turned right," Riefkohl notes. "One destroyer was then crossing starboard to port. The one crossing from port to starboard may have been an enemy, but as the two vessels barely missed colliding and did not fire at one another it is believed that they were both friendly. One DD (de-

stroyer) on our starboard hand, probably *Wilson*, was observed firing starshells and what appeared as heavy AA
machine-gun fire."

Riefkohl turned *Vincennes* hard right in an effort to
escape. It was not hard enough. Blazing down her starboard
side (more so than port) the stricken warship went into her
turn. Three torpedoes from *Chokai* sundered her No. 4 fireroom at this moment. Chief Water Tender Ianwicki picked
himself off the deck and reported that No. 4 fireroom was
flooding. On the bridge, Commander Loker was in the process
of sending a man to the engine rooms to see what was
happening down there. By the time the messenger returned
the ship had been hit.

"Both engine rooms are black and dead," Loker was told.

Chief Signalman George J. Moore, on the bridge all through
the action, saw the ensign shot away from the yard. Moore
quickly got another and braved the enemy shot and shell
to run it up. The flag stood out vividly in the glare of
flames and Mikawa's gunners, thinking it was the flag of an
admiral, redoubled their efforts to pummel *Vincennes* to
oblivion.

Dense smoke and flames curled from the below-deck spaces,
making it impossible to send down relief parties. An 8-inch
had made a shambles of the machine-gun platform, where the
dead lay in blackened heaps. Bridge ladders, ripped asunder,
were burning furiously, and the men trapped above had to
save themselves by rigging lines and coming down hand over
hand. Fire Controlman Wiggs (FC 2/c) and Lieutenant
Commander Craighill worked together here getting the injured
down to the next deck. It was this pair which found Commander Mullen, his leg broken by the concussion of the torpedoing.

Seaman Second Class G. R. Ferguson, standing topside
forward, found a bucket and began dipping water from over
the side. In control forward, despite the fact that all guns
were out of commission and communications were gone,
Lieutenant Commander Adams stayed at his post. At his feet
lay an unexploded Japanese shell. Directly below, a 1.1 clipping room was erupting thick clouds of smoke and steam,
but Adams remained calm. With him was I. N. Wingate, FC
2/c (Fire Controlman Second Class).

On the 5-inch No. 1 gun the two sole survivors of the
entire gun crew—Ensign R. Peters (a Reserve) and Platoon
Sergeant R. L. Harmon, USMR—fired on the conning tower

of a submarine reportedly surfaced about 400 yards away and made a hit, although this could never be confirmed.

By now Mikawa had passed on, as abruptly as he had arrived, and the *Vincennes*, a flaming derelict listing to port, was dead in the water. She had taken such a pounding as had few ships in history: 85 major-caliber hits.

Now began the job of collecting the wounded and preparing the rafts. Elsewhere in the stricken vessel, last-minute details required attention. In main radio, Pay Clerk Willess got the order to "prepare to abandon" and had his men jettison the coding equipment. He personally removed the disbursing records. In the pilot house, Commander Loker locked all confidential codes in the ship's 400-pound safe. The general signal book and signal vocabulary on the bridge was weighted and thrown overboard. Captain Riefkohl, his orderly Corporal J. L. Patrick, and Chief Yeoman L. E. Stucker then left the bridge.

On deck, life rafts were being released (in some cases chopped from their slings). Commander Mullen, with a broken leg, was lowered onto a raft by Lieutenant R. J. Badger. He wore Badger's life jacket.

Vincennes was listing sharply now and the sea began to spill over her deck as the rafts splashed overboard. Milton Schneller, EM 1/c (Electrician's Mate First Class), who had played some football before the war, found the door at the end of a passageway leading to the deck jammed and further blocked by the body of a shipmate, Chief Electrician's Mate Alfred Fergerson, who was struggling with the handle.

"Get out of the way! We're sinking!" Schneller shouted. Fergerson did not move. Schneller drew back about 20 feet and headed for a running jump at the chief's back, hitting Fergerson with his shoulder. The door bounced off its hinges and crashed on deck. Schneller then carried Fergerson to the railing in order to revive him in the fresh air.

Among the last to leave the ship was Dr. Samuel A. Isquith, who had been down in the after dressing station treating casualties. He remarked:

"When I had taken care of the last man, I opened the dressing station door and called out to topside asking if the order to abandon ship had been given. There was no answer. Dead silence. The deck, I noticed, was now listing about a 25-degree angle. I ordered my detail and casualties topside.

"A fierce fire was raging amidships. I could see that the *Vincennes* had only a few minutes' more floating time in her.

The whole superstructure was rapidly rolling over on her port side. Her deck guns were awash. We got the wounded into the life jackets and, one by one, helped them down the side into the water on the port side. By this time the blazing superstructure had begun to crumble. Flaming beams toppled to the deck, cutting off my own escape on the port side. At the same time, shells began exploding in the ready boxes.

"I hurried across the deck to the starboard rail and poised for a dive. I felt something sear into my right knee. I plunged into the dark water some 20 feet below, narrowly missing the after starboard propeller blade. When I came up, I tasted oil. Far off to my left I could see our sister ship, the *Astoria*, flaming amidships, silhouetted in the sky. . . ."

Captain Riefkohl and his orderly and chief yeoman reached the main deck near the No. 4 5-inch gun. Aware that the *Vincennes* was about to plunge, Stucker and Patrick sped fore and aft, respectively, to tell anyone remaining to jump clear at once. Riefkohl crossed the ship to starboard to do the same, and then returned to await his men. By this time the decks were canted sharply to port and water was sloshing about their knees.

"All right," Riefkohl said calmly. "It's all over. Let's go."

The three men pushed their way to the railing and over the side. For a few moments they swam hard to clear the pull of the sinking ship.

With the bodies of 300 officers and men still aboard, the *Vincennes* went down. She rolled over with keel up, and then twisted sharply downward by the bow in a cacophony of hissing steam as the waters of Savo Sound reached her boilers. It was 2:50 A.M.

CHAPTER 15

DEATH BOARDED the destroyer *Ralph Talbot* at the end of the battle. Lieutenant Commander Joseph W. Callahan (Annapolis '26) found Death standing beside him as Admiral Mikawa's cruisers moved around Savo Island. Gone were the *Quincy* and *Vincennes; Canberra* and *Astoria* were on their way to the bottom. Now only one tiny ship barred the path of the fast-moving Tokyo Express.

Admiral Mikawa saw the *Ralph Talbot* as no particular obstacle. A few shells would take care of it. He dispatched light cruiser *Yubari* of his inside column (*Yubari-Tenryu-Furutaka*) to smother the destroyer, while his force moved out at high speed. The main course had been eaten and found delightful by all. *Talbot* was just an after-dinner drink, to be sipped and savored. . . .

Callahan, thirty-nine, who had heard *Patterson's* warning at the outset, and had seen flashes of gunfire on the horizon, had taken off to the southwestward in the belief that he would catch up with the battle. He didn't. It caught up to him. As Callahan's radar swept around, ominous flashes of light from burning ships slowly inflamed the horizon.

"Boil up!" Callahan roared, and the single-stack, 341-foot lightweight sped toward the light that moved ever closer. He picked it up first at 28,000 yards. *Talbot* was already at battle stations. Nearing Savo Island at 25 knots, with searchlights and gunfire roaring on the horizon all the while, the destroyer skipper observed an intense exchange between two forces. Three American cruisers were now suddenly silhouetted by red floating flares. *Ralph Talbot* slowed. Callahan's hair stood on end. Those ships were afire!

At 2:15 A.M. a single searchlight flashed out over the waters on the *Ralph Talbot's* port bow, about 15,000 yards away. It played on the destroyer for ten long seconds and then swung away. Callahan and his bridge crew breathed easier, but only for a moment. The distant vessel's well deck

111

was burning and Callahan thought there was something familiar about the silhouette. He didn't think long, however. In
the next instant the stranger trained out his secondary battery and a rain of shells found the *Ralph Talbot*.

A hit wrecked the No. 1 torpedo tube and killed two men.
Callahan squinted at the colored dye in the powder splashing
over his ship—a color used by the U. S. Navy. A chill swept
down his spine, and he lunged for the TBS set in the house.

"Knock it off! Cease firing! You're killing your own men!"
Callahan shouted. The firing ceased abruptly and the *Ralph
Talbot*, already realizing this was no place for her, highballed
it out toward the western end of Guadalcanal. But the battle
wasn't over for Callahan's ship.

Three minutes later Mikawa had finished off his night's
work, and a good night's work it was. At this moment his
lookout perceived the tiny dark shadow of the *Ralph Talbot*.
Mikawa sent a blinker tube message to Captain Masami Ban
of the light cruiser *Yubari*. Three words flashed across the
darkness:

"Dispose of that."

Callahan's lookouts detected the enemy at the same time.
The *Yubari* was heading westward and crossing the destroyer's
stern from port to starboard. Two searchlights blinked on
even as the tin can's director fixed a yellow blob of light
moving across the screen. Now the *Yubari*'s secondary battery
and after turret opened fire, and the game of hide and seek
was over. As shells screeched down on the *Ralph Talbot*, the
radar range was read at 3,300 yards. Callahan raced out to
the open bridge, shouting for counter-illumination. It was
an order given just too late, for the searchlight wires had
been liberally sprayed with shrapnel not a moment before.

"Right full rudder! Torpedoes to starboard—fire!" Callahan
roared.

Three torpedoes charged at the *Yubari*, but only three. No.
1 tube had been put out of action in the earlier moments of
the *Ralph Talbot*'s two-phase battle. Now shells smashed
into the chart house under the bridge, partly demolishing the
port gun control system and setting this area ablaze. Other
shells screamed in to sunder the No. 4 gun and kill and wound
its crew. One gouged into the wardroom, and a moment later
flames were licking their way along the companionway leading
topside. Callahan turned his ship to port.

"Torpedoes to port—fire!" Here again the firing system had
been knocked out, and only one torpedo could be launched

by local control. The enemy searchlight focused on the after 5-inch gun. In a moment shells came in a hailstorm to batter this weapon into silence and blow two of the men over the side. Meanwhile, *Ralph Talbot* had developed a hard starboard list (20 degrees) and Callahan realized there was only one thing to do: head toward Savo Island.

Flames licked upward from the wrecked chart house and the signal bridge, where flagbags had ignited. A spectacular blaze was in progress and Callahan, hoping somehow to save his ship, managed to withdraw. *Ralph Talbot* was seriously crippled, with 23 wounded, twelve dead, and two missing. Her tiny sickbay was crammed full, and there doubtless would be further casualties if Callahan chose to turn his tin can into an abattoir. He didn't.

In the end a rain squall mercifully drenched the decks of the blazing ship. The enemy snapped off the searchlights and vanished. Callahan, who had tangled with a tiger and been whipped beyond dispute, was glad to see them go.

The *Yubari*, finished with her aperitif, sped away to rejoin Admiral Mikawa's forces.

For the destroyer *Helm* the night proved thoroughly unrewarding. Lieutenant Commander Chester E. Carroll, after the battle had opened, received orders from Captain Riefkohl of the *Vincennes* to attack. Attack what? So muddled was the radar screen that "the *Helm* remained ahead of the formation for a few minutes, then headed south." As Carroll hauled off, the three cruisers were seen to be taken under fire, but no targets had yet been discerned. Carroll, still moving, exchanged shots with a target which quickly identified herself as friendly.

The destroyer doubled back. By now the three cruisers were burning brightly. Carroll was stumped. His bewilderment increased as shell splashes threw up columns of sea ahead of his ship. Again, at 30 knots, he headed his destroyer south, and in the process of this high-speed sweep missed the enemy completely. The *Helm*'s total expenditure of 5-inch ammunition was four salvos—all of them fired on the friendly ship! If she had tried, Carroll's tin can couldn't have been of more comfort to the enemy than she was, at the conclusion of the battle.

Destroyer *Wilson* did little more. Lieutenant Commander Walter H. Price picked up Mikawa's force at 12,000 yards and promptly banged out two salvos. Because of the angle imposed, his guns wouldn't train. Price came left and reopened fire. For a lightweight, it was a goodly amount of fire. *Astoria*

was visible, in flames. *Wilson* aimed on the enemy searchlights. With the searchlights out, the destroyer turned and
headed toward Savo Island when TBS told Price that one ship
was standing out to the north of the island. He moved on at
30 knots, nearly colliding with *Helm* after firing some 200
rounds of 5-inch.

"No torpedoes were fired because of the confused nature
of the action," Price was to note. "No opportunity arose in
which the 20-millimeter guns could be used."

So it went.

But a grimly humorous battle remained to be fought
between *Chicago* and *Patterson*—a duel of two ships with
tight nerves and itchy trigger fingers, both steaming to
succor the stricken *Canberra*. It was a battle in which neither
ship was hit and which fortunately didn't last very long—
just long enough to give both sides a good scare. Hardly
had the salvos of *Chicago* and *Patterson* begun falling when
gunners recognized the familiar silhouettes of the "enemy."
With catastrophe narrowly averted, both ships returned
their attention to the *Canberra*.

Admiral Mikawa? Having finished the job on the Allied
screen, that worthy then focused his attention on the next
problem: what to do with the transports? His ships were
heading northeasterly on parallel courses. What to do?

"There was an enemy cruiser burning brightly far astern
of us as we ceased fire," Captain Toshikazau Ohmae records.
"I entered our operations room on *Chokai* and found it
peppered with holes from shell fragments. Had the 8-inch
[*Quincy's*] shell been five meters (fifteen feet) forward, it
would have killed Admiral Mikawa. . . . I asked the lookout
if there was any sign of pursuing ships. There was not."

Mikawa assembled his staff to discuss the transports.
He wanted to strike a real blow—sink the transports—but
was desirous of the concurrence of his staff. At 2:30 A.M.
the decision was made on the following considerations:

"1. The force was at 2:30 divided into two groups,
each acting individually, with the flagship in the rear. For
them all to reassemble and reform in the darkness it would
be necessary to slow down considerably. From their position
to the northwest of Savo Island it would take 30 minutes
to regain formation, another half hour to regain battle speed,
and then another hour to again reach the vicinity of the
enemy anchorage. The two and a half hours required would

thus place our re-entry into the battle area at five, just one hour before sunrise.

"2. Based on radio intelligence of the previous evening, we knew that there were enemy carriers about 100 miles southeast of Guadalcanal. As a result of our night action they would be moving toward the island by this time, and to remain we would only meet the fate our carriers had suffered at Midway.

"3. By withdrawing immediately we would probably still be pursued and attacked by the closing enemy force. But by leaving at once we could get further to the north before they struck. The enemy carriers might thus be lured within reach of our land-based air forces at Rabaul."

Admiral Mikawa's staff was jubilant. A great victory had been won, clearly won. The strategy of the Imperial Navy in emphasizing night gunnery had paid off beyond the wildest dream. There was only 35 dead and 51 wounded in *all* the ships of the force, and some of the vessels had no casualties whatever! They had expended 1,020 rounds of 8-inch ammunition in the process. Battle damage was incredibly neglible: a chart room burned out on *Chokai;* one of *Aoba*'s torpedo nests hit; on the *Kinugasa* shell holes in a storeroom and a few hits on her No. 1 engine room; one of *Kako*'s float planes downed with its crew. But that was it—Mikawa's *entire* battle damage.

The staff's decision came down in three minutes, and the admiral abided by it. At 2:33 A.M. his signalmen sent the order: "All ships withdraw."

Then, a fraction of a minute later: "Force in line, course 320 degrees, speed 30 knots."

CHAPTER 16

AT THE height of the battle, Admiral Crutchley was back aboard the flagship of the screening force, *Australia,* laying plans for an early-morning evacuation of the invasion unit. He had gotten no word from radar pickets *Blue* and *Talbot.* So far as the bearded Australian was concerned, 5 A.M. was the hour for reforming and pulling out.

"There had been no contact report from these [*Blue* and *Talbot*] ships or from *any* ship, and whilst being confident that our five 8-inch cruisers then on patrol could be sent against the enemy," Admiral Crutchley said later, "I was completely in ignorance of the number or nature of the enemy force and the progress of the action being fought."

Night of confusion! Night of horrors! So it went, from one monumental blunder to another. Even during the blasting of his warships, Crutchley was to order destroyers blithely to form around the flagship off Guadalcanal. Five of them would unscramble a garbled message and comply.

At 1:46 the admiral saw Japanese flares over the transport area. He took these to mean precisely nothing more than an enemy plane lighting the area. A moment afterward Crutchley saw a burst of light fire off to the southward, and interpreted this as some ship's AA batteries trying to knock down the intruder. When heavy fire soared out minutes later, Crutchley was not alarmed, and quickly returned to planning the evacuation.

Forty minutes later the Australian admiral took another look at the horizon. Sure enough, there was an awful lot of shooting out there! Crutchley went up to the *Australia*'s bridge and unzipped the TBS. At 2:26 a call went out to the *Chicago*:

"Are you in action?"

"Captain Bode, who had gotten his bow almost knocked off, came back with what amounts to the understatement of the year:

"Were, but not now."

Crutchley snapped out a call to the *San Juan*. Admiral Norman Scott's force, idle throughout the fight, had not been called upon to leave its north-south patrol between Guadalcanal and Tulagi. Undoubtedly Scott had heard the rumbling of guns, but since the OTC (officer in tactical command) hadn't pulled him off station, he wasn't about to do so himself. Scott replied:

"This force not in action. Appears to be surface force between Florida and Savo."

Crutchley call *Vincennes* several times. He tried *Quincy* and *Astoria* in turn. No answer. He asked *Chicago* to report the situation.

"We are now standing toward Lengo Channel. *Chicago* south of Savo Island. Hit by torpedo slightly down by bow," Bode unhappily reported. "Enemy ships firing to seaward."

The admiral's beard stood on end.

Bode's voice crackled over the airwaves: *Canberra* burning on bearing 50 five miles from Savo. Two destroyers standing by the *Canberra*."

Crutchley addressed a message to Turner, aboard his flagship *McCawley*, who must have been nearly out of his mind wondering what all the shooting was about out on the water. On the minesweeper *Southward*, Vandergrift wondered too. He was tired and haggard, in no mood for idle speculation. He contacted his command post for the latest information. The CP, recipient of a recent mesage from Turner, reported:

"Heavy enemy fire on Beach Red."

Vandergrift wanted to know more.

"Enemy attacking Beach Red in force," said the next message. Vandergrift, whose forces were about to be dumped on Guadalcanal to shift for themselves, was frantic. Marine radiomen tried to raise the flagship to find out more details. No answer. Was it a counterlanding? As this thought dawned in troubled minds, the firing on the water increased. One force was to the north, one to the south, with the former evidently catching it in lively fashion.

Vandergrift nearly popped his fuse as he now read a third message from the *McCawley*: "Enemy landing on Beach Red right now."

Someone ordered the duty officer to go down to the beach "to see if it were true." Meanwhile, a "battalion was alerted to make a counterattack in case the Japs really were landing." *McCawley*, in any event, would answer no questions. Vandergrift, who probably had some harsh words for Turner when told that the Marines were being dumped ashore on their own in the morning, was beside himself. It wasn't long before the patrol was back. Report: no landing. Vandergrift grunted a few choice words and retired to his cabin. It was no longer his concern.

Admirals Turner and Crutchley now had the exclusive worry over who was doing all this shooting, to whom. Actually, they knew little more than the Marine general. What about the destroyer pickets *Ralph Talbot* and *Blue?* What had happened to the radar on these ships? In his day order book the captain of the *Vincennes* had remarked: "The enemy can reach this position any time during the midwatch." These words had now come true, for "alarmist" Riefkohl's cruiser was resting on the bottom of Savo Sound.

Indeed, death had missed the *Blue* this night by less than 3,000 yards! Commander H. N. Williams was guarding on a line west of Savo Island, patrolling on courses 51 degrees and 231 degrees true, at twelve knots. During the midwatch the quartermaster had logged: "Weather partly cloudy, wind four knots from NE. Sea calm, visibility three miles. No moon," and nothing more.

The ship's radar worked well enough that evening. For one thing, a Japanese reconnaissance plane was picked up as it circled Savo Island and some of the *Blue's* crew claimed even to have seen running lights.

At 4:15 the destroyer had seen the flashes, first from the starshells and then from the patrolling ships. Tracers and heavy gunfire had soon boomed out from the black horizon. Williams had no idea what this was all about. If the enemy had penetrated—and evidently he had—then the logical conclusion was that he had come in from a different approach. Certainly no enemy ship could pass through these portals!

Or could they? It stands to reason that the operator on the radar set was the best man for the job. Moreover, Williams was aware of the enemy alert—that a force of ships was moving down The Slot. This was the reason why he was on picket duty in the first place.

Mikawa and every last man on his ships had held their breaths as they slipped by Williams' destroyer. A thousand guns were trained on the *Blue,* ready to blow her out of the water if there were any indication that the American had seen them. Commander Williams and his apparently sightless crew were diverted by a small two-masted schooner headed northeasterly. This vessel was overhauled and proved to be somewhat less than formidable—an inter-island tramp carrying coconuts and a native crew.

"At 2:50 sighted unidentified ship rounding Cape Esperance to the southwest at about average speed," Williams noted. "Trailed and closed until 3:25, when ship was identified as *Jarvis* enroute for repairs. Returned to station and resumed patrol. Sky becoming overcast and visibility closing in."

Destroyer *Jarvis* was blasted to pieces in the morning. Until *Blue*—the ship which had come so close to Mikawa and didn't sight him—received a call from Comdesdiv 8 to go to the assistance of *Canberra,* Commander Williams remained on station, "patrolling." Fate had given his tin can a singularly strange role in the fantastic Battle of Savo Island.

Destroyer *Bagley,* of the Southern Force, had been in action briefly. Although her torpedo primers had not been inserted quickly enough, Commander George A. Sinclair had somehow come around and fired four fish. Lieutenant John H. Gardiner (a Reserve) had seen one explosion in the enemy area two minutes after firing, while Edward Ryan, TM3/c (Torpedoman Third Class) followed these torpedoes with sound gear and reported four explosions about two minutes after firing. What these were is undetermined.

Mikawa, always secretive, did not mention torpedo hits in his report of this battle.

By 3 A.M. a small string of urgent messages deluged Admiral Turner's radio shack: *"Chicago* hit by torpedo, down by bow. . . . *Canberra* afire and sinking, destroyer standing by to remove survivors . . . . Have engaged *Nachi*-class cruiser. . . . *Nachi*-classers standing away to northeast. . . ."

Turner was thunderstruck. Where the devil were the *Saratoga, Enterprise* and *Wasp* now?

Vice Admiral Fletcher, proceeding at high speed with his carriers toward the southwest, was retiring without having yet obtained Admiral Ghormley's permission to do so. Turner now addressed an urgent message to him: "Surface action in Tulagi-Guadalcanal area." All possible assistance was requested. Fletcher, leaving the matter entirely to Rear Admiral Noyes of his staff, closed his eyes.

In command of the *Wasp* was Captain Forrest Sherman, whose air group had trained in night-fighting tactics. Three times Sherman asked Noyes to go to Fletcher and request that he turn around, for if a strike were quickly launched there was a chance to catch the enemy in The Slot. Also, the planes would furnish air cover for Admiral Turner, and nail Mikawa. Only *Wasp* and a few well-fueled destroyers were required. Noyes, possibly feeling as did Fletcher, declined three times. The matter was closed.

This was the break of a lifetime for Gunichi Mikawa. His greatest fear—that of carrier attack—was now irrevocably removed. It became official at 3:30 A.M. when Ghormley's consent to retire was received. Ghormley had no conception of what was actually happening to his invasion. He had only Fletcher's word that the carriers were in jeopardy and that air strength had been reduced in two days of fighting. His consent to Fletcher's retirement was given on this basis.

Meanwhile Turner, on learning of this decision, gritted his teeth and turned to salvaging his decimated forces. Mikawa was needlessly burning up fuel in his mad rush up The Slot, unaware that no carrier planes would haunt him this morning. He was as safe as a fox in an unlocked hen house.

Patterson, the destroyer which had broadcast the warning of strangs ships entering the harbor, steamed toward the stricken *Canberra.* Aboard her were nineteen dead and wounded. She had been severely mauled in the early part of the battle but now, at 3 A.M., was ready to help another ship *in extremis.* Commander Walsh, the executive officer who had taken Captain Getting's place on the *Canberra* when the latter lost consciousness on the bridge of his ship, requested that the *Patterson* come along the windward side amidships and furnish hoses for fighting fires. A second later this was amended:

"You had better wait."

American destroyermen could hear the sound of internal explosions coming from the bowels of the one-time pride of the Australian Navy. Commander Walker, heeding Walsh's words, sheered off in the darkness, to return when the all clear was given.

Helm and *Wilson,* to the southeastward of Savo Island, were directed by TBS to pick up survivors within a four and a half mile area. These were to be predominantly men from the *Astoria.*

Blue, sighter of an inter-island tramp schooner, closed the *Patterson* at full steam to assist the *Canberra.*

Bagley steamed to the assistance of the *Astoria* and, before dawn, would remove 450 survivors, including 185 wounded, from the burning cruiser. She would also pick up survivors from *Vincennes* and *Quincy*.

In addition, the *Mugford, Ellet, Hopkins,* and *Buchanan* would steam to the battle area. It was still dark, and in the water there were nearly 1,000 men.

CHAPTER 17

In the darkness the survivors swam and prayed. Savo Sound was warm, with a thick oil scum, and clogged with the debris of the dead ships. Small knots of life rafts floated together, the seriously wounded and the burned having been put aboard earlier, while the uninjured swam alongside. A shark watch was maintained by strong swimmers, who positioned themselves at the four corners of the rafts and some 75 feet outboard of them. Religion came easy.

Chaplain Robert M. Schwyhart of the *Vincennes,* whose last civilian pastorate two years before was the First Baptist Church of Kansas City, found himself in the water offering solace to three members of the engine room who had just floated off the *Vincennes.* It was at this moment that she shuddered in her death throes and rolled over. A life jacket, Dixie cups, toilet paper and pieces of lumber drifted by. Schwyhart talked slowly, quietly. At the end one of the men told him: "Padre, thanks for the words, but I'm still scared stiff."

"So am I," Schwyhart replied without hesitation. The men became separated soon after. Chief Yeoman R. L. Bigelow swam to Schwyhart's aide and together they came upon Ensign Robert Carter, who had commanded one of the 5-inch guns. Now he held fast to one of the cast recovery booms that had floated off. Carter made room for the new arrivals, saying, "It ain't much, but it's better than grabbing oil."

In the darkness the chaplain felt the body of a man bumping against his legs. He called out: "Come on up here with us. Get a hold of the boom." When the man didn't move, Schwyhart turned and saw the sailor's head immersed in the water. For a half hour the set of the current held the dead man against Schwyhart's legs. Finally Carter and Bigelow helped shove the body under the boom, and after this it disappeared.

Three life rafts welled up in the Stygian night, crammed

to overflowing and half submerged under the weight of many painfully injured survivors. Captain Riefkohl was there, clinging to one side. He had swum there with Stucker and Patrick.

"Who's there?" Riefkohl called out.

"This is the chaplain," came the reply. Evidently Schwyhart wasn't heard, for the commanding officer of the cruiser hailed him again. Again the response, "This is the chaplain!"

"Good boy!" called Riefkohl. "We can use you here."

Many of the men were moaning in agony, but many more were beyond moaning. Drs. Isquith and Newmen were in this group, unable to do more than say, "It'll be okay. Shrapnel comes out easy." Shock victims were unable to speak, and the men who had been burned bit the ropes holding the rafts together to keep from screaming. There were comics, too, who concealed their pain and fear with light banter. A storekeeper told a quartermaster:

"I'll bet a bottle of Four Roses would go for about two hundred bucks right now."

"Naw!" the other grunted. "Two thousand."

A fireman called out to Riefkohl: "You know, Captain, you never were a great one for granting liberty."

Lieutenant (jg) R. J. Badger was in the water too. He had found Commander Mullen, the exec, lying helpless near the catapults with both arms riddled and a broken leg. Badger had removed his own life jacket and forced it on the injured man. *Life* photographer Ralph Morse, the only civilian aboard, was in this group. He was saying it was a hell of a night to be caught without a camera.

Lieutenant Commander Craighill, with a half-dozen men who had combed the ship for wounded, made it away just as the *Vinny Maru* rolled over. They were here too. From the 5-inch gun decks came Lieutenant H. Barton, W. K. Wiggs, FC 2/c, and S. T. Jorgenson, S 2/c, after a tussle to free a snarled raft. In all, there were 200 men in this knot of misery and, before long, they would be joined by others.

When the *Vincennes* dipped her bow for the last time, these survivors saw the burning *Astoria* off in the distance. By the garish light of her flames their own ship's propellers, thrashing impotently in midair, stood out in bold and terrible relief. It was a sight never to be forgotten. In the water were nine of the cruiser's 24 colored hands, one boy with a "hole in his back the size of your fist."

Schwyhart heard a voice cry out, "I'm going, Padre! Say a

prayer for me!" By the time the chaplain swam to the spot, the sailor had made good his statement and disappeared. As the minutes passed and the fires from the *Astoria* did not diminish, the men began to speak of the other cruisers and, somehow, all the terrible suffering seemed bearable. On a raft, Warrant Officer Edward "Pop" Forster, a "plank owner" who had been aboard *Vinny* since her commissioning, closed his eyes and told a shipmate that the hole in his side didn't hurt any more. Pay Clerk Willness, nearby, idly wondered if they'd ever get the records straight.

In the last group to leave the ship was Milton Shipley, SK 2/c (Storekeeper Second Class), who had managed to bring along his searchlight. Now and then the light would blink in blind signal to attract anyone swimming nearby. Isquith, the dentist, noticed the light and after some time noticed that it was coming from three rafts lashed together. Almost 100 men were packed shoulder-to-shoulder here.

"I swam around the rafts twice, searching for a place to hang on. Every inch of space was occupied," Isquith noted. "In some spots men were lying on top of one another. Among them were wounded survivors. Exhausted, I decided that there was nothing to do but remain in the water."

Here were V. T. Barry, EM 1/c (Electrician's Mate First Class) and H. H. Stuart, CEM (Chief Electrician's Mate), so covered with oil that one of them nudged a colored mess attendant who was hanging onto a raft. "Move over, brother," he said. "We're in the same parish now." It was a long night.

"Knock off signaling, you sonuvabitch!" someone called from the water. "There are submarines around here!"

Across the water there were bobbing rafts from the *Quincy,* where Lieutenant Commander H. B. Heneberger was surprised to find himself senior surviving officer. Enemy shells had ploughed through that cruiser's house and chart room, killing all hands. Lieutenant Commander John D. Andrew, gunnery officer, had led a group of badly shaken men from the control platform to the rafts. In his report Andrew would commend Ensign Abe Francis Cohen for swimming out and saving several men who were without life jackets.

Lieutenant (jg) James C. Smith, in charge of a 5-inch gun, found himself in the water with about 50 men. All hands were trying to support themselves on a floater net, which was securely tied up in a roll and in a canvas bag. It was never removed from the bag, although the survivors tried long to get it out. As a result, many of these men were drowned. There also was Lieutenant (jg) T. A. Chisholm, a junior aviator who had served two years aboard the *Quincy*. In his report Chisholm would bitterly say:

". . . It is my opinion that the value of the five planes aboard it [*Quincy*] were not worth the hazard they presented. There is a possibility that on this type of ship two planes might be employed successfully to observe gunfire and carry out anti-submarine patrols, but they still offer a definite hazard to the ship."

Lieutenant W. A. Hall, Jr., (DC) was there. The young dentist, although severely wounded himself, had saved another man's life during the battle, by applying a tourniquet to the stump of a leg held against his own stomach. Hall would become a legend after tonight. And there were Lieutenant Commander C. F. Morrison, Lieutenant W. W. Forbes and F. P. Cohen, Ph. M 3/c (Pharmacist's Mate Third Class) who, while swimming in the oil scum, were to keep the rafts together and attempt to give first aid to the more serious cases. The rafts offered a grim hope to those in the water. As quickly as a man died, his body went overboard and another survivor would crawl from the waters of Savo Sound to take his place.

While the rafts drifted along, the men from *Vincennes* watched the burning ammunition dumps on Guadalcanal and Tulagi. No attempt was made to swim there. Nor to Savo Island, thought to be harboring Japanese and savages.

A few men from the *Astoria* (some injured) were in the water, lowered on orders from the executive officer. Lieutenant (jg) V. P. Healy had gone down a line into Savo Sound as early as 2:37, when the smoke and flames of the gutted cruiser isolated hundreds of men on the fantail. He swam until he joined a group of men trying to extinguish a blaze in a life raft. Only four rafts remained, the others having been shot away. Life jackets, stored on deck and down below, were burned in the *Astoria*'s fires.

To the south, where *Canberra* lay burning, the destroyer *Patterson* decided to risk another attempt to come alongside. The *Canberra* was listing to starboard from the torpedo hit in her boiler room. A light rain, which had begun as a fine drizzle, now had developed into a torrential downpour in this area. Lieutenant Commander Walker, the destroyer's skipper, decided it was time to do something for the Australians, despite her acting commanding officer's, "You had better wait."

Now there was no waiting. The downpour was of some help but, little by little, flames were to consume the *Canberra*.

Her ammunition stowage lockers amidships were exploding with catastrophic violence, sending flames, tracers and smoke roaring into the lightening sky. Sea and wind had heightened around the stricken ship. Nevertheless, destroyerman Walker nosed his ship close enough to pass hand billies and hoses. It was 4:08 A.M. when he began the evacuation of wounded from the *Canberra* via cargo nets, brows and small boats.

(In all, Walker would remove about 400 survivors, including 60 wounded; the destroyer *Blue* an additional 250.)

An hour later Commander Walker's radio shack received the lugubrious report that the *Canberra* was on her way to eternity. The message was from Admiral Turner, and it said: "IT IS URGENT FOR THIS FORCE DEPART THIS AREA 0630." In the next minute came another message: "IF *Canberra* CAN NOT JOIN RETIREMENT IN TIME SHE SHOULD BE DESTROYED BEFORE DEPARTURE."

Walker, who had come to assist, now became the bearer of horrible tidings. Commander Walsh, perhaps sensing this might eventually happen (his ship had a seventeen degree list and fires raged about her decks and below decks—really out of control) accepted his fate.

It was during the abandonment of the *Canberra* that the short-lived duel between the *Chicago* and the *Patterson* took place, after which things again became "normal" and the evacuation continued. Destroyer *Blue*, meanwhile, had been ordered in from her peaceful stamping grounds to assist. Mikawa's battle had passed her by during the night. (Although spared in this action, the *Blue* would succumb of a torpedo hit in fourteen days.)

At 5:50 A.M. the sun climbed over Cape Esperance, and its appearance was enough to thrill the men still in the water to the north of Savo Island. "How wonderful to be able to see the light of a new day!" Chaplain Schwyhart said. Many of the men on the rafts offered prayers, while others simply stared at the sun and shook their oil-matted heads. A coxswain was heard to tell a boatswain's mate soberly: "Jesus Christ, that thing's pretty!"

It surely was. And the higher it rose, the more beautiful it became. For with the sun came destroyers—first moving over the horizon, then, after an interval, coming closer. A blinker light flashed out at the men on the rafts, and on one of them Chief Signalman George J. Moore read slowly:

"There is an enemy submarine in the near vicinity. Keep

yourselves out of the water as much as possible, because we are going to drop depth charges."

The rumbling of fifteen depth charges wafted across the water. Schwyhart noted: "There was a terrific force striking us from all sides. But there were no ill effects."

Not long after, the life rafts bounced alongside the destroyers *Wilson, Ellet* and *Mugford,* which were hove to and lowering cargo nets. Schwyhart relinquished his hold on the recovery boom and struck out with the rest. "There was a line within arm's reach and with it I pulled myself to the net and climbed up. Upon setting foot on the deck of the destroyer *(Mugford),* all my strength left me. I couldn't walk, so I sat down for a few minutes. Soon I went into the galley, and a ship's cook gave me a cup of black coffee. Needless to say, it was good. I have never tasted such coffee."

For all the survivors there were coffee, cigarettes, fresh water, and something to eat if a stomach could hold it down. The three destroyers, crammed to the gunnels with wounded, moved into the anchorage and put 682 men aboard the transports *Barnett, Neville, American Legion, President Jackson* and *Hunter Liggett.*

But these were the men of the *Quincy* and *Vincennes.* There still remained question marks behind the names *Astoria* and *Ralph Talbot.* Where was Callahan's plucky destroyer? Easy. She was dead in the water, her black gang working furiously to get two boilers back on the line. Her topsides had been shot and burned away, her radio was dead. Yet later that morning Callahan would bring his fighting junk heap back to Tulagi.

At 8:30 Admirals Turner and Crutchley received a radio message from the destroyer *Selfridge.* She and *Ellet* had combined to consign the *Canberra* to a watery grave. Together they had fired 268 rounds of 5-inch and a half-dozen torpedoes, mostly faulty. Finally, it was the *Selfridge* who advised Turner that the *Canberra* was sunk. A torpedo had taken her MOT (middle of target).

Able Seaman Murray was to speak of this moment later: ". . . Our hearts ached as we gazed back at our old ship, now slipping fast over to starboard. Fires were still burning, ammunition still exploding, smoke still belching out of many a jagged shell hole. Vale, *Canberra.*"

CHAPTER 18

Astoria's END had commenced hours before. Admiral Mikawa's abrupt departure left Captain Greenman with a flaming coffin, dead in the water, its inter-communications gone, and with 150 men—without life jackets—on her fantail, waiting for an abandon ship order.

Fires raged below decks as well as in the superstructure. Towering flames leaped into the black sky. The bridge was a shambles. Captain Greenman, wounded by shrapnel, was advised by Gunnery Officer Truesdell to leave the bridge, as machine-gun bullets were exploding above. Some 300 casualties had been brought forward on deck.

"I looked down on the fo'c'sle and saw the wounded lying there—and I prayed," Greenman told the veteran correspondent Custer. "I prayed to God it would stop."

Greenman sent his executive officer, Commander Shoup, below to round up the other men. The exec went down a line to the main deck and fought his way tortuously through the fire and smoke to the fantail. Turret 3, still manned, had no power except manual. Shoup kept it manned in the event Mikawa should return. *Astoria* shuddered under the impact of a violent explosion across the water. *Quincy* was gone, the victim of her own internal explosions. Fearing the same fate for *Astoria,* Shoup quickly ordered a few men into four rafts and lowered away, with orders to stick together.

In Turret 3 were empty 8-inch powder cans, enough for a good many rafts. Crewmen were sent to bring back all that they could find. Lashed together, these cans could save lives. Shoup now conferred with Lieutenant (jg) Blough, the officer in charge of Turret 3. Were the magazines hot? They were not, Blough told him. The exec was relieved.

"I ordered him to keep a watch in the handling room, and if any evidence of fire nearby appeared, he was to flood them at his descretion," Shoup noted.

On deck, the fires were being fought by ingenious men

who tied lines to powder cans and scooped up sea water. As Mikawa's massed gunfire had smashed the main risers almost at the start of the battle, their fire hoses were useless. Curiously, it appeared that *Astoria* was holding her own.

Lieutenant Gibson, an engineering officer, staggered out from below decks. Smoke had nearly felled him, but after a few moments in the fresh air he had encouraging words for Shoup. Gibson offered hope and sound advice. The engine rooms and firerooms were intact, he told the exec. If the fire could be restricted, it could be licked. Even the gods conspired to assist the *Astoria* at this point. A rain squall raced over the area and deluged the fiery hulk. On the boat deck, the fire appeared to be coming under control.

Lieutenant Commander Hayes, the engineering officer, made up a repair party and began work on the starboard side of the hangar. Here, too, the firemen were winning their battle. The repair party advanced to the well deck, all the while bringing under control numerous blazes. Now they found another huge fire raging in the galley and one in the lumber hold. These were oil-inspired infernos, which were extremely dangerous and difficult to manage. Neither CO_2 nor water helped. Two unconscious and burned sailors were found in this area. And here was seen a hand waving feebly, the body apparently wedged between the starboard forward whaleboat davit and the break of the upper deck. The victim was trapped. C. C. Watkins, Sea 1/c (Seaman First Class) shoved his extinguisher at a shipmate and dashed through the flames. He reached the wounded man but, because of the former's position, soon needed help.

Wyatt J. Luttrell, SF 3/c (Ship Fitter Third Class) and Norman R. Touve, WT 3/c (Water Tender Third Class) bounded from the repair party. They brought back the first victim, then noticed another clinging to the armor belt. Passing a line to him, the three men quickly hauled this sailor to safety. This was heroism of the highest order, and it would later be recognized. There were other instances—many others.

Another crew chose to go below deck. C. Brower, BM 1/c (Boatswain's Mate First Class) and several other men joined Topper, supervisor of the watch when the shells began falling, in a dash to the sail locker to look for life preservers. "All buckets, mattresses, life preservers and any material that could be used for first aid was passed topside," Topper was to say later. To this officer the *Astoria* was worth saving, despite a bonfire running down her length from the navigation bridge aft. "I returned to the forecastle and had men cut up all cordage that could be found, to use for life lines in the event we had to abandon."

In the darkness a ship appeared close by. It was destroyer *Bagley* of the Southern Force, attracted by the roaring bonfire. Blinker lights winked across Savo Sound and a cheer went up from the *Astoria's* battered crew. The can moved in closer, port side aft. But suddenly she stopped. Lights flashed again and *Bagley* went full reverse. Her soundmen had detected the presence of a Japanese submarine in the area, and she was off to drop a pattern of depth charges.

"Go get him!" A shout went up from the *Astoria's* crew.

When *Bagley* returned, a "Chinese landing"—starboard bow to starboard bow—was made, and all hands proceeded to leave the *Astoria*. Her fires and the threat to her 5-inch magazines were too much to cope with, and Captain Greenman did not believe she could be saved.

Crowded to overflowing, the *Bagley* again backed off.

Five minutes later a light blinked out from Astoria's fantail. There a small knot of men were seen. Immediately Captain Greenman, despite his wounds, gave the order to stop the *Bagley* and reverse course.

As the *Bagley* again approached the dying ship, Topper and Andrew, standing on the deck, peered anxiously into the dawn, trying to estimate the extent of the *Astoria's* damage. This now became manifestly clear: the fore and aft trim appeared normal; the three-degree list was unchanged; her armor belt had eight large holes above the waterline; but this was all. Of course, the rest of her superstructure and the entire topsides were ablaze.

"So what!" an engineer snapped. "We can save her."

Now was gathered a resolute group of men—artificers, engineers, signalmen and radiomen—as the destroyer closed *Astoria's* fantail. Captain Greenman announced his intention to stay with the ship until they had saved her.

On this note, a titanic job was begun. Three hundred men volunteered for the job. With Greenman, they boarded the stricken cruiser. *Bagley* withdrew to a safe distance. Three fire-fighting parties were organized to combat the blaze. Shoup was assigned the grisly job of finding all the bodies and moving them forward for a mass funeral. Corpses, shot up and burned beyond recognition, were taken to the foredeck, where a sailmaker began sewing them up in canvas. The dead bodies were then weighted with shell casings. Pharmacist's mates went about collecting the identification tags. (Later the box in which these blackened momentos of Savo reposed was lost.)

Hayes went below, as he had hoped to do before the cruiser was abandoned. Engineering personnel fought their way to the engine rooms and to No. 3 and No. 4 firerooms. Because of the debris and fire on the main deck, Hayes couldn't get his crew into No. 1 and No. 2 firerooms. In No. 3 boiler room, No. 5 boiler was burned up for lack of water; No. 6 boiler, in the same room, was too hot for careful examination. In No. 4 fireroom there was fuel oil in the bilges.

Battery power was gone, battle hatches to both engine rooms were blown off their hinges, but, generally speaking, Hayes was rather pleasantly surprised.

Topper went below with a damage control party to inspect the deck spaces aft of No. 2 engine room. He reported: "We found all hatches, drains and ventilation valves closed. A five-inch hole had been plugged in the starboard side of D306L, and this was holding very well. A 5-inch shell had pierced D308L and passed into D-10F without exploding. Fuel oil could be seen through this hole. It was plugged. . . . . We found a couple of weepy rivets in the GSK storeroom. The smoke in these below-deck spaces had cleared up considerably. Some small smoldering fires were extinguished in the 3rd Division part of the ship."

On deck, Lieutenant Walter Bates donned asbestos gloves and went into a compartment where there were two unexploded enemy shells. He calmly tossed these over the side.

And so it went. Captain Greenman was to say in his personal report: "Instances of amazing personal courage and devotion to duty were observed, and beyond question of doubt those who died at their posts gave their last effort without thought of personal danger."

Ashore, Admiral Turner now had scant hope of making the evacuation deadline. He realized this even as he dispatched destroyers *Wilson* and *Buchanan* to the *Astoria's* aid. From Tulagi came the fast minesweeper *Hopkins* to take the *Astoria* in tow. Was there *still* hope? *Hopkins* passed an electrical lead over (wrong size) to *Astoria's* engineers, and waited orders to commence towing. These never came.

It was a losing fight. At 11:30 the men of the *Astoria* began to sense that they were whipped. First, the fire which raged in the wardroom, and below the wardroom, defied all efforts to be brought under control. Then a magazine in the forward part of the ship blew up. The result of the fires and the explosion was a noticeable increase in the degree of list. Slowly the waters of Savo Sound began to enter the ship.

The list increased. Down below, exhausted members of the black gang asked their officer what was holding up the works. Hayes had no idea. On deck, Shoup was beginning to realize that all was lost. Sickly yellow gas fumes curled from the forward space where the magazine had exploded. Blood-soaked, sweat-soaked crewmen worked with a desperation born of the knowledge that their ship was sinking.

The hole at Frame 80 and the other at Frame 60, port side, could not be plugged. On the fo'c'sle, Captain Greenman knew it too. He watched in sick amazement as the destroyer *Wilson* suddenly backed off. Lights had blinkered to the *Astoria*'s signalman, communicating regrets. Now appeared the transport *Alchiba* to offer a towline, as *Hopkins* dropped hers. The exec, Shoup, came up with the sad news that nothing was going well any more. *Astoria* was sinking and Greenman —with eleven shrapnel wounds—and the remnants of his valiant relief crew would have to prepare to abandon.

Ensign Mullens, a "90-day wonder," was below on deck with a mattress cover tied around his bleeding face. He was one who insisted on remaining. Up forward, rending sounds of metal meant that bulkheads were finally giving away. There was another explosion up forward, and more ominous rumblings.

Topper, aft, felt the hatch handle leading to the 5-inch store. It was hot to the touch. He worked his way to Captain Greenman to tell him what he thought. If the magazine went, most of the men in that area would go too. Greenman gathered about him the key men of the cruiser—Shoup, his exec; Topper, his first lieutenant; and Hayes, his engineering officer. The concensus was unanimous.

"Call in the *Buchanan*. We will abandon," Greenman said softly. Lieutenant Gibson, a deck officer, went forward with a group of men to the starboard bow. The list had grown to 30 degrees, and it was now evident that the *Astoria* wouldn't last more than another few minutes. *Buchanan* came in to about 300 yards of the cruiser, waiting. Small boats came down from the destroyer and from the transport *Alchiba*.

The 8-inch powder cans, lashed together for this eventuality, were gently pushed over the side. As they splashed in, many lines were lowered from the *Astoria* to the water. Two rafts were already tied to the ship, and as the crew began dropping into the water the rafts were seen to float free. Among the last to leave the dying ship were Topper and Greenman. The decks were slanting almost at 45 degrees as they walked the length of the ship, ordering crewmen over. There was no rush to leave. Men simply lowered themselves down lines, hit the water with a splash, and then came up and struck out for the small boats moving in toward them.

It was 12:15 P.M. when *Astoria* heeled over to port on her beam ends and sank. Captain Greenman, now aboard the *Buchanan,* watched her go.

CHAPTER 19

IT WAS "a sad Sabbath" for Admiral Turner's forces. The exodus began a few hours after the *Astoria* slipped beneath the surface of Savo Sound. At 4:10 the Coast Guard-manned transport *Hunter Liggett*, acting as guide for Transport Group X-ray, put to sea and shaped for Noumea, New Caledonia. In her cramped living spaces were the survivors of the three American cruisers.

Ahead lay a four-day, 1,000-mile voyage and at its end, for Turner, a lengthy conference with Vice Admiral Ghormley. Few who stood on the decks of ships, as they steamed out of Lengo Channel, stared across to the beachheads. It was enough to know that the Marines were there. The immediate concern was the care and comfort of the wounded, and there were many. For ships' doctors the grueling work of stitching up bloody, torn bodies had begun. Isquith of the *Vincennes*, a survivor aboard the *Barnett*, was called upon. He borrowed a pair of pajamas, grabbed a cup of hot coffee, and reported to the operating room. Cohen, the pharmacist's mate, was another man who pitched in to help.

Schwyhart, chaplain of the *Vincennes*, was aboard the *Barnett* too. He commented later: "I saw, in the wardroom, my duty. Everywhere, on the decks and on tables and chairs, were severely wounded officers and men."

The orgy of fiery destruction was over. Those who had survived were going home.

Signalman K. P. Meyer of transport *Jackson*'s C-Division was one of hundreds in the force who dumped the contents of his seabag on deck and said aloud: "Take what you want, fellas. Just leave the snapshot of my kid." The crews gave everything—shoes, scivvies, dungarees, shirts, even toothbrushes. On the *Fuller*, carrying a number of *Astoria*'s oil-blackened survivors, a chief storekeeper unlocked a supply closet and observed: "If you don't find it here, you won't find it anywhere."

134

The crews of the destroyers and transports extended their sympathy to the point where sleeping quarters were turned over to the survivors. Up on the flag bridge, flagbags became highly sought night places. Sailors curled up anywhere... in gun tubs, behind transmitters, behind engines. The word was "wake me when it's time to go on watch." Stripping of foot lockers for the benefit of survivors was the order of the day.

On some of the ships there were men beyond help. There were those who died soon after climbing the cargo nets, and some who lingered until the last day of the voyage. Captain Getting was one who never made it to the hospital ship *Solace*, waiting in New Caledonia. These casualties of Savo, weighted with a 5-inch shell and sewed into a Navy blanket, were put over the side after a simple ceremony.

Aboard the *Barnett*, crowded with survivors from *Canberra* and *Vincennes*, there were 179 operations in a sixteen-hour period. An Australian pharmacist's mate, with shrapnel still in him, shrugged off his continuous duty in the operating room. "They need me in there, cobber," he said firmly.

On the flagship *McCawley*, Admiral Turner was sweating out the long voyage home. He was within range of submarines and, for all he knew, bombers. He had a report waiting for Ghormley that would curl his hair. The deadline set by Turner for departure had been missed by ten hours, during which time crews worked tirelessly unloading a few tons of supplies (25% of all cargo in the transports) for embittered Marines. Turner probably wondered why Japanese bombers didn't come down that Sunday, but until the end of the war the answer to this question would be locked in enemy files.

Admiral Yamada of the 25th Air Fleet at Rabaul had sent down a flight—sixteen bombers—which was diverted at the last minute to sink a crippled "*Achilles*-class cruiser" limping in the general direction of Australia. This was the destroyer *Jarvis*, whose death ironically had saved Turner's transports from Parthian attack.

Admiral Turner was not likely to forget the Solomons. Nor Savo Sound—now Ironbottom Sound—where four first-line cruisers were resting on the bottom. Nor was he apt to forget Admiral Fletcher for his strange role in the affair. If Turner felt sorry for anyone, it was General Vandergrift, the unsung hero of Guadalcanal. His forces had been dumped ashore on strange islands and told to shift for themselves. The Marine general, Turner realized, would have plenty to say later.

And Vandergrift? For a few hours the Marine general was bitter. Then, almost philosophically, he dropped the matter. Correspondent Richard Tregaskis, bouncing in a jeep between Kukum and Matanikau, had heard "scuttlebutt" about a great sea battle fought during the night. Soon thereafter he went down to Beach Blue.

"There was no official word on the matter at Marine Corps headquarters," Tregaskis noted, "except that the Australian cruiser *Canberra* had been sunk." Not even Prime Minister Curtain of Australia knew this much.

If Vandergrift had anything to say about Turner's exodus that Sunday afternoon, he would get it said on paper, and later. At present he had real problems to cope with. He was short on supplies, without air or sea cover, and subject to severe counterattack which was definitely on the way. A logistical hot potato had been dumped in Vandergrift's lap and the only way to solve it was—do it himself. On Guadalcanal there were 11,148 Marines instead of 15,000, and on Tulagi there were 6,805 instead of 4,000, because the Gavutu fighting had proved far more intense than intelligence revealed.

While Vandergrift was preparing to deal with this business, Vice Admiral Ghormley in Noumea was anxiously awaiting the arrival of his invasion forces. He had a thousand questions to ask Turner and Crutchley. He couldn't understand why Fletcher had retired, in view of the situation confronting Turner. Nor could he understand why Fletcher, hearing of the attack on the cruisers, had not turned around and launched an air strike. How many men had been lost? What was the current situation in the Solomons?

Vandergrift could give him an earful!

And what of Crutchley? Ghormley wondered. Where did the bearded admiral go during the battle? Crutchley, who had won a V.C. for valor in World War I, was not a man to shy from a fight.

Ghormley got the answers soon enough.

Meanwhile, Admiral Mikawa was on his way home to a rousing *Banzai* welcome at Rabaul. As soon as his force assumed cruising disposition, Mikawa radioed his "estimated dawn position" so that Eleventh Air Fleet planes could "strike any pursuing enemy carrier."

Ohmae recounts, "Detailed reports were soon coming in from each ship concerning results achieved." Admiral Mikawa particularly wanted to know of the damage sustained and the munitions expended. "Reported claims came to a total of one light and eight heavy cruisers and five destroyers sunk; five heavy cruisers and four destroyers damaged ... we estimated finally that five enemy heavy cruisers and four destroyers had been sunk."

What a night it had been! Beneath Mikawa's happy façade, however, was a deep and nagging fear of enemy carrier planes. In *Chokai*'s plotting room, Ohmae and his colleagues attempted to figure how long they would have to be under way before they were safe from retaliatory strikes. Long enough, they guessed.

"The hours passed, and no enemy planes were sighted," Ohmae avers. "There was no indication at all of the enemy carriers whose transmissions we had heard so loud and clear on the previous afternoon. It was reassuring to know that we were not being followed, but our spirits were dampened by the thought that now there would be no chance for our planes to get at the enemy carriers."

On this greedy note Mikawa, at 10 A.M., split his forces south of Bougainville and ordered Crudiv 6 to highball for Kavieng. A good night's work was done.

Only one bit of shooting war was yet to take place while Turner was still at sea—*S-44* vs. *Kako*. It occurred far north of Turner's position, and did little to avenge the defeat, except in a broad sense.

Early Monday morning the Crudiv 6 force—*Kako, Aoka, Furutaka* and *Kinugasa*—were standing in for Kavieng base as they had done before the Savo raid. The seas were calm, and the morning breeze barely riffled the surface, so that a periscope could sight, and be sighted, a long way. Japanese gunners were probably polishing brightwork and hanging out the flags for the triumphal homecoming, for they were too busy to see the periscope that Lieutenant Commander J. R. "Dinty" Moore poked aloft at 7:50. Only 850 tons, and the product of the World War I building program. *S-44* was making her third war patrol from Brisbane. Her hull leaked; her engines sounded like an old percolator. But her skipper wasn't one to notice minor inconveniences.

Moore sighted the first ship at 9,000 yards; the second and third in a column a few moments later. He brought his submarine around for an 80-degree track, then quickly changed his mind as he saw a fourth cruiser. He made rapid calculations for gyro angle, depth and range. Meanwhile the first cruiser sped by. The second and third were good set-ups, but the last was it.

Outer torpedo doors were open. The range moved down. Moore counted the seconds. Range was 700 yards, zero gyro angle . . . ready. *Fire!* Four torpedoes lunged for the *Kako*. The first two missed, the last two took her amidships.

"You could hear hideous noises that sounded like steam hissing through water. The noises were more terrifying to the crew than the actual depth charges that followed," Moore noted. "It sounded as if giant chains were being dragged across our hull, as if our own water and air lines were bursting."

Moore made no attempt at an "end-around" to get in front of the remaining cruisers and fire torpedoes again. He couldn't. He was down to 130 feet and rigged for silent running. Mikawa, hearing of the *Kako*'s torpedoing, began to hate American submarines. Needless to say, in time he would come to hate them a good deal more.

But the S-44 incident didn't take the joy out of the Battle of Savo for Mikawa. Probably it jarred him a little, because his own Eighth Fleet submarines were having notoriously poor luck around the Solomons. But, beyond this, his homecoming was abounding in *Banzais!*

Turner's was not.

When the transports arrived at New Caledonia on Thursday, Ghormley was waiting. First there was the removal of survivors to a base hospital and hospital ship. Then there was the matter of clothing and "ditty bags" for men who had lost everything. Finally, Ghormley and Turner had a lengthy series of talks. Crutchley, who had undertaken to offer an explanation while still aboard the *Australia*, wrote: "The fact must be faced that we had an adequate force placed with the very purpose of repelling surface attack; and when that surface attack was made, it destroyed our force."

This candor was soon to be misinterpreted.

Japanese news broadcasts, heard in London, bewildered the American public. Newspapermen were beginning to bombard the Navy Department; Admiral King was hard put for something to say. In Pearl Harbor, Admiral Nimitz closed his mouth tightly and took a target pistol out to his private range. When he returned in an hour, he was his usual self-possessed self.

All ships present except the *Jarvis* submitted action reports. While the Navy Department studied them, newspapermen pounded at Admiral King's door. The Navy allowed as how enemy attacks were "in force" and that "severe resistance from land-based aircraft is being encountered." But nothing more was admitted.

Admiral King, meanwhile, was reminded in the press of his obligation to the American people. So were, in fact many other persons in high office. The Navy (King) still declined to give answers. But Turner said his piece to Ghormley, and in writing. The latter, in turn, attempted to explain to Nimitz. Ghormley's error was being 1,000 miles from the fighting front. This was really minor when compared with the many tragic blunders that took place a few minutes after Mikawa's float planes dropped their flares. What about Fletcher? Why did the *Blue* fail to give a radar report? And why did Captain Bode of the *Chicago* not give warning to the North Force?

Nimitz demanded answers, and before long the Commander in Chief of the Pacific Fleet would have enough to write a book. *Life* photographer Morse was flown to Pearl Harbor for a series of secret conferences with Nimitz, and Fletcher was on his way to explain his now-famous diffidence. Five years hence, Professor J. T. Dorris would compare the defeat at Savo to the loss of the Spanish Fleet at Manila Bay, in *Log of the Vincennes*. It would be a comparison by a man who had lost a son in the plotting room of the *Vincennes*. Dorris would draw a very correct analogy between the immolation of the Spanish Fleet, commanded by Rear Admiral Topete, and that of the Allied Fleet under Vice Admiral Ghormley.

Admiral Nimitz now summoned to Pearl Harbor a few of the key commanders of Operation Watchtower, in an effort to get to the bottom of the Solomons disaster. The reluctance of the Navy Department to discuss Japanese claims of a stunning victory in the Solomons Island was nearing an end.

CHAPTER 20

For Admiral Nimitz, Commander in Chief of the Pacific Fleet, the Savo jigsaw didn't fall neatly into place until September. By this time there were answers from Ghormley, Crutchley, Fletcher, Turner and Vandergrift. Action reports, submitted by all ships in the battle, likewise were in his files. Admiral Nimitz was now able to draw a perfectly muddled picture of where responsibility for the defeat lay.

Fletcher's answers, among the last to be received, revealed nothing particularly startling. The carrier admiral, fingered by every field commander, justified the withdrawal of his force on the basis that all carriers were "equally low" on fuel; and to the presence of many enemy torpedo bombers in the area. There was some question in Fletcher's mind whether the Mikawa force could be caught in The Slot without a daylight reconnaissance. His earlier reason for withdrawing—reduced fighter-plane strength—stood.

Nimitz saw his duty. Fletcher, having just tangled with Admiral Nobutake Kondo's carriers in the Solomons, in an action which almost saw the loss of the carrier *Enterprise,* was to be relieved of his command. It was a painful decision to make, for Fletcher had been in every engagement since the beginning and had done extremely well. His star had shone at Coral Sea and Midway. The carrier admiral had mauled Shima at Tulagi, to the point where the latter's invasion force was virtually wiped out.

Fletcher Pratt, biographer of the Marine Corps, summarized the general reaction to Admiral Fletcher's lack of initiative. He wrote:

"He was a tired man, not with the local tiredness of seventy-two hours on duty, like the crews of the cruisers, but with the accumulated fatigue of many months of the most arduous command in the war."

Admiral Nimitz turned in a preliminary report, then a more comprehensive report, to Admiral King. Operation

Torch was coming up in Europe and King, occupied with numerous details of the gigantic Allied offensive, turned the Savo business over to Admiral Edwards of his staff for further investigation. In December Admiral Hepburn, former Commander in Chief of the Atlantic Fleet, conducted a more detailed inquiry for Secretary of the Navy Frank Knox.

In the meantime another battle had been fought in the Solomons, and Vandergrift's Marines were bracing for the battle of their lives as General Hyakutate, 17th Army chief, prepared to throw two full crack divisions into Guadalcanal. It was not exactly a secret that something had happened in the South Pacific. Australia knew about Savo almost immediately, and officially on August 20 when Prime Minister Curtain made the sad announcement of the loss of the *Canberra*. Even in the jungles of Guadalcanal the men were aware "there was a lot more to that gunfire on August 9 than headquarters was willing to admit." Japan, in her glorious effort to advise the world of Savo, sent a twin-engine Mitsubichi over the Matanikau to drop a copy of the *Greater East Asia Newspaper, Special Edition* for our newspaper-starved Marines.

Tregaskis speaks of finding "a highly colored report" in which Japanese editors claimed:

"Sunk: battleship (unknown type)—1; armed cruiser (*Astoria* type)—2; cruisers (unknown type)—at least 3; destroyers—at least 4; transports—at least 10."

American newspaper readers became aware that something had gone wrong at Savo. Every day monstrously exaggerated Tokyo reports (heard in London) appeared in the nation's press. Still no word of the catastrophe from the Navy Department. King wanted all the facts. Further, he wanted to keep the enemy guessing.

By October Admiral Edwards had pieced together the salient facts of the incredible debacle, and Admiral Nimitz elected to make some command changes in the South Pacific. Admiral William "Bull" Halsey was brought in to take Ghormley's place, and Admiral Thomas Kinkaid, a battleship admiral, moved into Fletcher's spot. By October, too, the Tokyo Express was wheeling down The Slot, bringing troops to Guadalcanal. There were new battles to interest the American newspaper reader, and gradually his attention turned from the Savo defeat. In the Solomons, the enemy was grooming for a year-long fight such as the world had never known.

Ghormley, before being relieved, had stripped his garrisons on New Caledonia and sent 3,000 men to Vandergrift in a convoy built around the battleship *Washington* and the carrier *Hornet*. Some 5,000 Marines from the Samoa garrison had been shipped as reinforcements.

Ghormley was not too surprised that lightning had struck him. He had somewhat expected there might be this reaction. Halsey, on the other hand, climbed into the saddle with "astonishment, apprehension and regret," for the two men had been friendly for some years.

On October 12, fully two months after the loss of the cruisers, the Navy Department released Communique 147, which stated: "Certain initial phases of the Solomon Islands campaign, not previously announced for military reasons, can now be reported . . . ." Whereupon it proceeded to give a clear, factual account of the battle.

The impact was as expected. Hanson Baldwin of the *Times*, twelve days later, wrote that the naval forces had been "surprised like sitting ducks." And he enumerated the surprises—patrolling in a fixed position . . . waiting for the enemy instead of hitting him . . . radar failure . . . communications failure . . . no decisive plan.

Crutchley, who was somehow to survive public wrath, possibly because his peculiar role was understood in higher echelons, also was criticized for his lack of battle plan. What, screamed the press, was an Australian doing in command of American naval forces? The wrath of the pen roared rampant. (On October 27, 1944 a second release concerning just the *Vincennes* was issued to radio stations, a sort of biographical sketch.) Turner emerged the hero, if any hero there was, and remained in the Pacific, advancing to four-star rank in 1945. For Guadalcanal, Turner received the Navy Cross: "While subjected to repeated severe air attacks and intense enemy opposition, Rear Admiral Turner led his forces in launching the initial attack and, due to his expert leadership, courage and determination, carried it through to complete victory. Further, by landing supplies and equipment, he insured the holding of the objectives captured for use in operations against the enemy."

Turner was a good deal closer to the battle than most realized. The cruiser *Astoria* had been his command in 1939. Ironically, she was chosen to transport to Tokyo the ashes of Hiroshi Saito, the Japanese ambassador to the United States.

Few men fared as well as Turner. Captains Greenman, Riefkohl and Bode (the last named at the end of the war) went to shore jobs, never again to take a ship to sea. Ghormley and Fletcher ended up in desk jobs in the States, Ghormley later going to Germany and Fletcher to the North Pacific. In Panama, Bode, depressed, went into his bathroom and shot himself. However, Greenman of the *Astoria* managed to survive the calamity surprisingly well. He attained the rank of commodore (a wartime rank) for his excellent staffwork in the Pacific. Riefkohl attained flag rank in retirement.

In the destroyer divisions, Callahan and Carroll achieved flag status. Both, upon retirement, advanced to rear admiral on the basis of combat awards—Carroll receiving his for his intrepid attack on Rabaul in 1943. Walker was less fortunate. The man who had cried, "Warning—strange ships entering harbor!" and then charged to the attack, retired as a four-striper, with a memory that was to last him a lifetime.

In Australia, smarting as this country was over Savo, there was a period of public indignation and shock. Curtain was under fire for withholding information (actually he released the news only eleven days after it happened), as was his admiral, Crutchley, for the shame of the *Canberra*'s tragic end. Eighty-four of a crew of 816 were lost. Although he had nothing to do with the sinking, Crutchley became the goat. Weeks later the British government acknowledged its debt to the Royal Australian Navy by turning over to it the 10,000-ton *Shropshire,* a cruiser of similar class. Mrs. Frank Getting, widow of *Canberra*'s captain, was present at the commissioning ceremony. She told reporters: "I am proud of Frank. He loved the sea and he was willing, if need be, to give his all for his country. He would not have wished to go any other way."

In Washington, Admiral King was drafting a report to the Secretary of the Navy:

> "The surprise which was the immediate cause of the defeat, was the result of circumstances. Because of the urgency of seizing and occupying Guadalcanal, planning was not up to usual thorough standards. Certain communication failures made a bad situation worse. Fatigue was a contributing factor in the degree of alertness maintained. Generally speaking, however, we were surprised because we lacked experience. Needless to say, the lessons learned were fully taken into account."

The hue and cry died down as other battles came to pass,

yet the American public was not allowed to forget. Representative Melvin J. Mass, (R) Minnesota, wrote his now-famous article titled "Mistakes I Saw in the Pacific—A Plea for Unified Command," for the *American Mercury*, in January, 1943, shortly before Admiral Hepburn completed his investigation. This did nothing to settle the nerves of the press.

In May, 1943 Admiral Hepburn filed his exhaustive report, a report which has since been classified as secret and is therefore not available for study. Admiral Samuel Eliot Morison, whose remarkable *History of United States Naval Operations in World War II* is a bible for students of naval history, had access to this report. Hepburn, Morison quotes, states that "the complete surprise achieved by the enemy was the primary cause of the defeat."

Summarizing Hepburn, he continues:

"(a) Inadequate condition of readiness on all ships to meet sudden night attack.

"(b) Failure to recognize the implications of the presence of enemy planes in the vicinity to attack.

"(c) Misplaced confidence in the capabilities of radar installations on *Ralph Talbot* and *Blue*.

"(d) Failure of communications, which resulted in lack of timely receipt of vital enemy contact information.

"(e) Failure in communications to give timely information of the fact that there had been practically no effective reconnaissance covering enemy approach during the day of August 8."

Morison, quoting Hepburn, states:

"As a contributory cause . . . must be placed the withdrawal of the carrier groups on the evening before the battle. This was responsible for Admiral Turner's conference . . . (and) for the fact that there was no force available to inflict damage on the withdrawing enemy."

As "cause for defeat was so evenly distributed," Admirals King, Nimitz and Hepburn agreed that "it would be unfair to censure any particular officer."

In passing, one cannot help but wonder what Admirals Ghormley and Fletcher might have thought of this statement.

Admiral Hepburn interviewed all persons concerned. No doubt he referred to the written action reports, in which case the recommendations of many officers present were taken into consideration. In any event, battleship linoleum and fleets of fabric-covered float planes soon disappeared from the Pacific.

Right here, one very pertinent point should be considered: The force that is surprised and beaten always looks bad—perhaps unjustly so. The surprise, if counteracted by a victory, paradoxically redeems these individuals whom newspapers and literary critics refer to as "the goat." Also it should be said that luck played a great part in the Japanese victory: luck regarding the elements of the sighting by an Australian bomber—two, in fact—hours before; luck in not having been found by McCain's aircraft; luck in the *Blue-Ralph Talbot* radar fiasco; luck in Captain Bode's failure to warn the Northern Force; luck that the weather in certain sectors was terrible and visibility was down; luck in the fact that the ships were at Condition II; luck that the enemy's potential was underestimated; luck that planes rested on catapults to light Mikawa's night; luck that Crutchley offered his men no real battle plan; and luck that Mikawa got away with murder.

And what of the Japanese admiral after he pulled into Rabaul? Captain Ohmae says in *Proceedings,* "Combined Fleet sent an enthusiastic message congratulating him on his success in this notable action." But apparently the loss of all those juicy transports bothered Combined Fleet, for they took Mikawa to task. Ohmae notes:

> "It is easy to say, now, that the enemy transports should have been attacked at all costs. There is now little doubt that it would have been worthwhile for *Chokai* to have turned back, even alone, ordering such of her scattered ships as could to follow her in an attack on the enemy transports. And, if all had followed and all had been sacrificed in sinking the transports, it would have been well worth the price the effect the expulsion of the enemy from Guadalcanal. . . ."

Savo had a particular meaning to the American people, and by December, 1943 this was translated into the commissioning of another *Quincy* for the Navy; in March another *Astoria,* and in January, 1944 another *Vincennes.*

CHAPTER 21

THE BITTER taste of defeat proved a blessing in disguise. It brought resolution and candor, cohesion and self-examination. Admiral Crutchley, later to command MacArthur's Navy (Task Force 44) was able to say: "The fact must be faced that we had an adequate surface force placed with the very purpose of repelling surface attack, and when that attack was made it destroyed our force."

In the wake of the Savo defeat, there was a period of bitter recrimination in the nation's press, and for a while in the Navy too. Although Admiral King and persons at the command level desisted from acrimony ("No officer should be held accountable for not anticipating the Japanese attack"— King's letter to Secretary of the Navy Forrestal, September 14, 1943), nevertheless there was plenty of acrimony, spoken and unspoken.

At BOQ's and the Royal Hawaiian bar, one heard talk comparing the attack on Pearl Harbor with the attack at Savo. If Short and Kimmel of Pearl Harbor fame had been taken to task and punished for that affair, why not the commanders of Savo? Wasn't Savo every bit as bad in some respects as Pearl? In 1945, when Captain Charles B. McVay III zagged instead of zigged and the *Indianapolis* took a fish, did that officer and gentleman get off lightly? He did not. Correspondingly, it was said, neither should the men at Savo be let off the hook.

But as the war was still in progress and it was wiser, all things considered, to let Savo lie, the matter was dropped. Not for long, however. In a year there would follow two tremendous blasts in big-circulation periodicals. Thereafter, Savo would keep cropping up in books at the rate of one every few years.

Admiral Turner, of all men at Savo, emerged in every sense a hero. The New York *Daily News* of February 25, 1945 reported a Tokyo Radio broadcast which denounced the Commander, Amphibious Forces, presently at Iwo, saying: "This man Turner must die!" The broadcast spoke of Turner as "being responsible for the killing of countless numbers of our own younger and elder brothers on various islands throughout the Pacific." This was certainly so, and Turner had no compunctions about doing it.

"This man Turner shall not return home alive—he must not and will not!" the broadcast concluded.

A few campaigns such as Midway, Saipan, Okinawa and Iwo Jima helped divert public focus from the Savo issue. Turner, a truly remarkable man, helped do it. At the age of forty-two, Turner had checked in to the Naval Air Station at Pensacola and asked for flight instruction. He had qualified a year later. Standing fifth in the class of 1908, manager of the baseball team, and editor of the *Lucky Bag*, Turner (born May 27, 1885) was essentially a planning officer with a reputation for plain talk.

As a point of illustration, a friend of Turner's once recounted that a general, superior in rank, had brought a military plan for him to look over. Turner ridiculed it and inquired, "Whose is it?"

"It's mine," snapped the red-faced general.

Whereupon Turner repeated his original opinion, holding his ground with more tenacity than tact.

Admiral King, upon the outbreak of war, thought enough of Turner to ask him to join his staff. How could a man like this be misled at Savo? The fact remains that he was.

The blasts of icy wind came first out of Chicago, where the excoriation of the United States Navy was high on the list of post-war grievances. The *Tribune* suggested that responsibility for Savo rested with two men. In an article entitled "The Savo Whitewash" (June 6, 1946) Colonel McCormick's big-circulation newspaper took Turner and Crutchley over the coals for the deaths of the men aboard the four heavy cruisers.

On August 16, same year, *Time* lowered the boom by calling Savo "the worst blue-water defeat in the U. S. Navy's history." *Time* said: "The reasons originally offered to explain how four cruisers were lost in a half hour in a night attack by the Japs still stood: human exhaustion, inexperience of command, failure of radar and of radio communications. In a foot-high stack of action reports, the Navy went no further. The new detail that did come out was an explanation of how the command afloat failed. Its mistake: Given ample warning of the approach of a powerful Japanese force, it failed to read the warning aright."

The *Time* article generally rehashed the battle, saying:

> "... When word of the losses trickled out, two months later, it made U.S. morale sag. The captains of the *Quincy* and *Canberra* had died with their ships. The captain of the *Chicago* died in Panama, apparently by his own hand. Riefkohl of the *Vincennes* and Captain William G. Greenman of the *Astoria* were never given more responsible commands.
>
> "Said Admiral Ernest J. King, 'In my judgment, those two officers were in no way inefficient, much less at fault. . . . Both found themselves in awkward positions and both did their best with the means at their disposal.' "

"But," concluded *Time*, "the stubborn fact remained: four great ships had been lost, with 952 U. S. officers and men and 84 Australians (1,023 correct figure). The Japs (it later developed) had a slight edge in ships and guns, but not enough to foreclose the decision. The crux of the matter was the misjudgment of what the Japs were up to. If the enemy's actions had been properly appraised, all the physical factors of human fatigue, poor visibility, unreliabile radar and stuttering communications might have been overcome."

J. T. Dorris of *Log Of The Vincennes*, whose loss was personal, brought up these pregnant questions in 1947:

Why didn't Crutchley tell Riefkohl of his departure for the meeting aboard the *McCawley* with Turner?

Why did we have a British commander in charge of so large an American force of ships? (The Chicago *Tribune* asked the same, in substance.)

Why hadn't the Navy court-martialed *someone* in connection with the Savo catastrophe?

The attacks continued without let-up. The leaders of Savo came under fire in Congress, on the radio and occasionally in the newspapers. Later in books. Essentially, these bombardiers all asked the same questions. Nothing was settled. Nothing would be settled, for the war ended in unconditional surrender. There was, to paraphrase Admiral King, no sense making scapegoats. The Navy lacked battle-mindedness then, but not later.

Though the Battle of Savo stands as a monument to inexperience, there emerged the most powerful naval force in the world which, in its just and terrible wrath, swept the Japanese from the Pacific.

CASUALTY LIST

Chicago	2 killed or died of wounds						21 wounded	
Canberra	84	,,	,,	,,	,,	,,	55	,,
Vincennes	332	,,	,,	,,	,,	,,	258	,,
Quincy	370	,,	,,	,,	,,	,,	167	,,
Astoria	216	,,	,,	,,	,,	,,	186	,,
Ralph Talbot	11	,,	,,	,,	,,	,,	11	,,
Patterson	8	,,	,,	,,	,,	,,	11	,,
	1023						709	

BIBLIOGRAPHY

Action Reports: *Vincennes; Astoria; Quincy; Chicago; Canberra; Ralph Talbot; Blue; Bagley; Patterson; Wilson* and *Helm.*

The Army Air Forces in World War II, edited by Wesley Frank Craven and James Lea Cate, University of Chicago Press, 1953.

The Coastwatchers, by Commander Eric A. Feldt, RAN, Oxford University Press, 1946.

Fleet Admiral King, A Naval Record, by Fleet Admiral Ernest J. King, USN, and Walter Muir Whitehill, W. W. Norton and Company, Inc., 1952.

The Great Sea War, edited by E. B. Potter and Fleet Admiral Chester W. Nimitz, USN, Prentice-Hall, Inc., 1960.

The Guadalcanal Campaign, by Major John L. Zimmerman, USMCR, U. S. Marine Corps, Historical Division, 1949.

History of the United States Naval Operations in World War II, Vols. IV and V, by Rear Admiral Samuel Eliot Morison, USNR, Atlantic-Little, Brown and Company, 1949 and 1951.

HMAS Mark II, published by the Australian War Memorial, Canberra, 1944.

A Log of the Vincennes, by Johnathan Truman Dorris, The Standard Printing Company, Louisville, Ky., 1947.

Midway, by Captain Mitsui Fuchida, IJN, and Commander Masatake Okumiya, IJN, United States Naval Institute, 1955.

Savo, The Incredible Navy Debacle off Guadalcanal, by Richard F. Newcomb, Holt, Rinehart & Winston, New York, 1961.

Mysteries of the Pacific, by Robert de la Croix, John Day Co., 1957.

Pacific Battle Line, by Foster Hailey, The MacMillan Co., 1944.

Samurai! by Saburo Sakai with Martin Caidin and Fred Saito, E. P. Dutton, 1957.

A Military History of the Western World, by Major General J. F. C. Fuller, Funk & Wagnall Co., 1956.

The Splendid Little War, by Frank Freidel, Little, Brown, 1958.

Through the Perilous Night, by Joe James Custer, The MacMillan Company, 1944.

Destroyer Operations in World War II, by Theodore Roscoe, U. S. Naval Institute, 1953.

Submarine Operations in World War II, by Theodore Roscoe, U. S. Naval Institute, 1949.

The Battle of Savo Island, by Captain Toshikazau Ohmae, edited by Roger Pineau, U. S. Naval Institute Proceedings, December, 1957.

Ships in Distress, by J. H. Adams, The Currawan Publishing Company, 1944.

The Silent Service, by T. M. Jones and Ion L. Idriess, Angus and Robertson, 1944.

The Marines' War, by Fletcher Pratt, William Sloan Associates, 1948.

Guadalcanal Diary, by Richard Tregaskis, Random House, 1943.

Battle Report, Vols. II & III, by Captain Walter Karig, USNR and Commander Eric Purdon, ISNR, Rinehart & Co., 1947.